Praise for *The Popping Cor*

This is the kind of book you pick up and cannot put down. The story line grabs you and doesn't turn you loose. It certainly does not disappoint. I fish those islands and was delighted to see the detail of description when introducing the reader to the beauty of this part of Florida...

—Captain Terry Vander Meer

Mr. Grant not only has created a "keep you guessing" murder mystery with plenty of colorful characters, but he has also given his reader an insight into life in Southwest Florida. The setting is perfect for this kind of story, complete with great descriptions of the laid-back lifestyle in a little town where nothing ever happens—well, almost never. This is a great book for the beach, or the pool, or in front of a warm fireplace. I can't wait for Mr. Grant's next offering.

—Carl D. Megill

Terrific read! Couldn't put the book down! This book has romance, suspense, and history rolled into one. Definitely recommend reading!

—Carol Faircloth

Praise for *The Cut Bait Murders*

If you enjoy a suspense story mixed together with a dash of history and a cup or two of humor that is shaken—not stirred—on an island off the southwestern coast of Florida, you will love Mitch Grant's latest addition to his Pine Island Mysteries. *The Cut Bait Murders* is a page-turning adventure, filled with characters who pull you along as they try to solve the disappearance of fellow islanders.

—Pati Vander Meer

Great read! Mitch Grant puts you in Saint James City and the rest of Pine Island. You could easily taste the island's food and drinks, and you become one with the residents…Mr. Grant also sticks in some history of the island but doesn't bore you. You want to be there. I loved it. Hurry up and write another book.

—"JuJu"

Praise for *The Silver Spoon Murder*

Here we go again! This book could not be any more current with the goings-on in Saint James City, Florida, today: threatened development and environmental concerns. Take those as the main issues, throw them in the pot, mix in a little mystery and murder, top it off with real historical facts that never bore, add in vibrant local color, and you've got another great book by Mr. Grant (who, by the way, lives on the island). I truly get lost in his books as the characters in them travel up and down the seventeen-mile-long island visiting all the local haunts and waterways.

—"JuJu"

I've read Mr. Grant's first two Saint James City Mysteries, so naturally, I couldn't wait for his third novel to come out. Needless to say, I wasn't disappointed. Although this novel deals with real-life environmental issues, his characters come to life and make the story even more real. There are many suspects to choose from who might have killed the environmental activist, and, to the end, Mr. Grant keeps you guessing. Jim and Jill Story are like a modern-day Nick and Nora Charles, and their interaction makes the story fun to read. All I can say is that I hope Mr. Grant is working on a fourth mystery.

—Carl D. Megill

I live in Saint James City, so I'm biased. I like it that I go to the same places as the characters in the book. Best of all, the book is a fast-paced, fun read.

—"Capt Clem"

Fantastic read. It is hard to put this book down. Hope we get more from this author—soon!

—Marsha Gale

Have I told you that I read Mitch Grant's books twice? Once to just enjoy the story—what, and who, was Jim Story after this time? The second read, I take my time and just enjoy the details. I especially love the sights and scenes of Pine Island Sound and the characters unique to the area. My first read of the book was this past summer. I have now finished my second read, and I must admit that I enjoyed this book as much the second time as I did the first. I can almost smell the salt air and see the mullet jumping...

—Pati Vander Meer

the
FLORIDA RIG MURDER

A Saint James City Mystery

MITCH GRANT

ISBN: 1539482065
ISBN 13: 9781539482062
Library of Congress Control Number: 2016917508
CreateSpace Independent Publishing Platform
North Charleston, South Carolina

This book is dedicated to my six grandchildren: Ainsley, Max, Carolina, Cooper, Christopher, and Hadley. I am so proud of all of you! Someday, when you are old enough to read this, I hope you will enjoy this story.

For me, reading has always provided a window to the world—offering unlimited access to knowledge, information, history, travel, entertainment, and life. I hope that you, too, will all develop a love of reading. Educate yourselves, and then go forth with wonder, honesty, integrity, humility, a thirst for knowledge, compassion, enthusiasm, and the courage and energy to act on your convictions. I love you all!

—Grand Dude

PROLOGUE

The man slouched against the boat's leaning post. He watched, without a great deal of interest, as the big center console piloted itself down Pine Island Sound. Truthfully, his mind at that moment was not particularly focused on the journey. Rather, he was reflecting on what had transpired earlier on the deserted Cayo Costa beach. And, as he did, he couldn't keep a grin from spreading across his face. Yes, he said to himself, this had certainly been a day to remember.

The woman lying facedown on the boat's bow, naked except for the strings of her thong, was having similar thoughts. And just thinking about him again made her breathe a little deeper, squirm slightly, and push her hips against the deck of the boat. But, knowing where these thoughts likely would lead, she consciously made herself exhale and tried to think about something else. She, too, was smiling.

She then lay still on the deck, enjoying heat from the sun's rays on her already deeply bronzed skin, luxuriating in what was effectively a massage as vibrations from the boat's hull soaked deeply into her tired muscles. This pleasure, she thought, was one of the reasons she'd always loved to be on the water. She'd just drifted off to sleep when the sound of a helicopter intruded. As she woke, she didn't know what she was more upset about: not being able to sleep, or not being able to continue the dream she'd been so enjoying. Regardless, she was annoyed. And now, what she most wanted was to sit up and use both hands to relay the universal "up yours" signal. But her mostly naked condition, and the little modesty she still possessed, prevented her from doing so—then.

The chopper's noise had stirred the man out of his reverie as well. Now, as he focused on the aircraft, he was glad he didn't recognize it or, as far as he could see, anyone in it. He didn't relish the thought of having to explain why the young wife of one of his farm's suppliers was lying nearly nude on the bow of what was unmistakably, unquestionably, his boat. He was also glad the woman had not made things worse by rolling over or sitting up. But that relief was to be short-lived.

The helicopter hadn't paused simply to admire the boat and its crew. Rather, it hovered for a moment along the craft's port side and then looped around to assume a similar station, moving at the same speed as the boat, along the starboard side. The woman had tolerated the first interruption, but this second incursion into her privacy was more than she could accept. She angrily sat up; turned her bare chest toward the noisy aircraft, which was no more than thirty yards away; put one hand under each of her distinctively tattooed, oversized breasts; and lifted them, as if to seductively present them for closer inspection by the chopper's pilot.

It was difficult to say, however, if the pilot actually enjoyed the presentation, as the helicopter soon departed, now flying in the general direction of Fort Myers's Miserable Mile channel. The woman, while glad the chopper had flown away, was just a little disappointed the pilot hadn't at least waved to acknowledge what he'd seen.

"Damn, Lois Anne, why did you have to do that?" the man shouted in the booming, irritating Hendry County drawl that was his trademark. "Why'd you have to show him your damned tits?"

The woman turned toward him and stuck her tongue out. She presented him with the same display she'd just offered the pilot and said in a playful, pouty voice, "What's the matter, honey? You're not the jealous type, are you?"

The man opened his mouth to reply, but the sight of her breasts made him reconsider. Finally, he just mumbled, at what was for him an uncharacteristically low volume, "You shouldn't have done that."

She laughed and then stared, almost challengingly, directly into his eyes.

The man shook his head and stared back, but this time, he wasn't looking at her eyes. After a couple of moments, he asked, "You in a hurry to get home?"

"Uh-uh," Lois Anne whimpered. She knew she didn't have to rush home. Her husband's flight wasn't due at Southwest Florida International until after eight.

The man turned the boat toward a deserted cove, thinking as he did that this day really *was* going to be one he'd long remember.

And he probably would have—if he hadn't been murdered.

Chapter One

Saint James City, Florida, is a small, quiet fishing village located, literally, at the end of the road. It's the kind of place you've got to *want* to get to in order to get there. The road in question, Stringfellow, dead-ends at the southern tip of Pine Island and was named to honor the long-deceased island resident and county commissioner responsible for having it built.

Pine Island is seventeen miles long, north to south, and only a couple of miles wide at its broadest point. Some claim it's the largest island in Florida. Without question, it's at least the largest "undeveloped" island in the state—a status the island owes to the farsighted efforts of a group of residents who, almost forty years ago, were successful in putting in place a land-use plan at the county level that effectively prevented large-scale commercial development. As a result, the island in some ways tends to resemble a place largely forgotten by time. And nowhere on the island is that truer than in Saint James City.

This village is one of the oldest communities in Lee County; in fact, it was the county's very first incorporated city. But that town, established near the end of the nineteenth century to capitalize on a nationwide tarpon-fishing mania, soon failed. Despite all the periodic real estate frenzies for which Florida is so infamous, Saint James City remains a tiny, unincorporated, largely unknown piece of "Old Florida." Sadly, it is one of the last such enclaves in the state. That's one of the reasons we moved here.

My name is Jim Story. Five years ago, my wife, Jill, and I retired from careers in banking and moved to Pine Island. My ancestors had come to Florida shortly after it became a state back in the 1820s; consequently, I can proudly claim to be a "cracker." Jill, not a Floridian by birth, can't make the same claim, even though she has spent the majority of her life here—she was blessed to have grown up in a tiny North Carolina mill town. During our careers, we had more than enough time to "enjoy" city life, and once we retired, we wanted to get back to our small-town roots. We also both tend to value privacy and have sometimes been accused of marching to the beat of drums that are, at the least, unusual. I guess those may be other reasons Saint James City appealed to us.

Having lived here for a while, we've come to believe that life in this remote village, and probably life in *any* remote village, is by necessity going to be different from what most would consider normal. And a corollary of that observation is that the character of the individuals living in any town located at the end of a road will probably, due to some process of self-selection, tend to diverge from the ordinary. And we further posit that when both of those geographic axioms are combined in a place as whacked-out as Florida, the likelihood, and magnitude, of these deviations will be enhanced considerably. And those, we have come to appreciate, are other reasons we so enjoy living here.

Saint James City has one miniscule grocery store, a few boat-yards, a tackle shop, a fish house, several marinas, two real estate offices, one church, a couple of restaurants, and five bars. All the bars are popular and successful. We have the American Legion post as well, which, unsurprisingly, also features a very busy bar.

Our little town has a permanent population of only a few hundred folks—a number that swells to easily four or five thousand during "Season." *Season* is the term everyone around here uses to refer to the time between November and April, when the weather up north is cold and miserable and the weather in Florida is, well, perfect. Those few of us who choose to live here year round tend to prefer the non-Season months. This is because, while we gladly welcome our winter visitors back each year, we understand that during this period we probably won't be able to get a table in a restaurant or a seat in a bar. Many of our full-timers—those who have to work for a living—depend on the cash flow that comes with the annual migration of "snow-birds" to our area. And, truthfully, we all enjoy having someone different to talk to. Life here during the summer months, while exceptionally pleasant, can sometimes also be a little lonely. And that, perhaps, is why many of us here spend so much time drinking and partying.

Before we retired, Jill and I led pretty tame lives. Granted, we'd often attend corporate events with clients, and we certainly enjoyed weekend nights out at favorite restaurants. But we were far from being party animals. Down here, though, once you're retired, every day is Saturday! I guess it's like an occupational hazard for retirees. It didn't take us long to realize that, if we were going to avoid developing problems with alcohol, we would have to pace ourselves. And we do try—Lord, do we try—but it's just not that easy!

For example, the bars in town take turns presenting bands or musicians, so there's someplace to go listen to quality music just about every night of the week. On the weekends, they *all* have music, sometimes starting at noon and continuing until…well, until long after dark. And it's not just that Jill and I are tempted by the well-played rock, blues, country, or zydeco. No, having lived here for a while, we've now gotten to know many of the performers on a personal basis, and we almost feel obligated to attend their performances. Who knew we would become groupies in our sixties?

Bar music is not the only temptation we have to contend with, either. In an isolated village at the end of the road, residents have to invent their own ways to have fun. Consequently, the art of the house party has been raised to a new level here. Everyone's bar is kept fully stocked, and every pantry has the makings of at least one easily prepared party snack. All that's required to get a party started is a good excuse, and on an island full of characters, excuses to party are not hard to come by. And the advent of social media has made the issuance of invitations, and acceptance of the same, almost instantaneous. Consequently, it's not unusual for us to have three, and sometimes more, parties a week to attend.

Like I said, it's not all that easy to pace ourselves in Saint James City.

And, as I also mentioned before, our little island has more than its share of characters. For starters, some of the island's full-time residents are descended from the folks who used to fish here for a living. Many of them like to call themselves "Mullet-heads," a term that has absolutely nothing to do with how they wear their hair. Rather, it's a reference to a local fish—a fish that at one time formed the basis of the economy on which their ancestors depended. Most of those folks have now adapted to life in the twenty-first century and are making good livings by providing goods and services to the snowbirds; however, a few are still struggling with making a successful transition, especially after a night of heavy drinking, and they tend to be the ones who provide many of our island's more colorful stories.

Another portion of the full-timers on the island are those who have retired here from elsewhere, attracted by the little piece of Old Florida at the end of the road. We tend, perhaps, to be slightly less colorful than the Mullet-heads, and a trifle more controlled, but we do try to do our part to uphold the island's reputation. For some reason, Ohio and Indiana are especially prevalent points of origin for many of these retirees.

The third and last major segment of our full-time population is that which I call "the Floridians." These are folks who lived their lives elsewhere in the state and were successful in their careers. They were able to build or buy second homes here, and when they retired, they elected to live in Saint James City full time. Those with a background in agriculture form an important subset.

Fifty miles to the east of Pine Island, in Hendry and Glades Counties, is one of the most productive agricultural regions in the entire country. This area is blessed with rich soil, an abundant supply of fresh water, and—critically—mild winter temperatures. Much of the country's winter fruits and vegetables come from this region. During the last century, farming in the United States wasn't all that profitable, but now, with our expanding population and shrinking supply of arable lands, that is no longer the case. Consequently, many of the largest homes on the island now belong to farmers, who also tend to own some of the most expensive boats around. Most of the farmers, as you would expect, given their rural roots, are good people. But, without question, a number of them are true characters. Jill and I feel blessed to call many of them friends.

Tonight's party was at the gorgeous back-bay, waterfront home of Georgia and Robert, two of our dearest friends on the island. Robert grows watermelons and tomatoes, but that simple statement hardly does justice to the scope of his farming operation, which I've been told (though not by Robert, who's far too modest to make such a claim) is the largest producer of early-season melons in the entire United States. Their parties are always fun.

Chapter Two

Jill had warned me that the party tonight—by Pine Island standards—was going to be a large one. Georgia and Robert were hosting the affair to celebrate the recent diagnosis that, after a long battle, Robert's body was finally free of cancer. We were delighted that we had been invited to share this occasion with them.

While we anticipated the party would be crowded, we were still surprised at the number of guests when we arrived. There must have been a few hundred! While Robert and Georgia's house is sizable and its screen-enclosed pool is massive, even this expansive space was insufficient to accommodate such a crowd. Consequently, the hosts had thoughtfully erected tents equipped with tables and chairs on the lawn. Alongside the walkway leading to the pool's entrance was a tent that sheltered a staffed bar, which was busily providing free beer to a large crowd of thirsty Pine Islanders. As we walked by this crowded enclosure, we stopped and chatted with a number of folks we recognized. But

the party's real action was inside by the pool bar. I was not surprised, as I knew this was where Robert's free, top-shelf liquor
was being dispersed. I impatiently steered Jill in that direction.

Once inside the pool screen, we noticed a band was setting
up. We smiled, knowing that Robert, without question, would
have booked the best band in Hendry County to perform. We
were looking forward to hearing it play. The next thing we
noticed, as we elbowed through the tightly packed throng, was
that the food was still being laid out. Georgia had told us earlier
that she had arranged for the island's best barbecuers to prepare the meat for the party: pulled pork and spareribs. We were
looking forward to tasting their handiwork. Apparently, so was
much of the crowd, as many had begun to line up in anticipation
of the dinner bell's toll. We kept moving, heading purposefully
toward the bar.

This location, as with any party, was where the real fun was.
The conversation here was louder, the laughter merrier, and the
bodies more tightly pressed together. We happily elbowed our
way in, hoping to find a magic passageway toward the harried
ladies serving drinks. As always, Jill proved more adept at the
required slithering than I, her 125-pound frame giving her an
obvious advantage over my more considerable bulk. She was soon
able to score drinks, light beer for her and a scotch and water for
me. Knowing Robert's taste in whisky, I had anticipated that the
spirit poured into my drink would be top quality, and I wasn't
disappointed. Once fortified with required refreshments, we
began to happily work the crowd.

Almost everyone we knew in town was at the party. The first
person we chatted with was the island's electrician, a great guy

named Eddie, who had helped us out with the many power-related issues we had encountered as we'd settled into the forty-year-old house we'd purchased. Eddie's a great fisherman, too, and unlike many islanders who just talk a good game, he has the pictures to prove it. We always enjoy hearing what he's been up to.

All the ladies who make up Jill's "canasta" (a.k.a. drinking) group and their husbands or significant others were in attendance. Since we see them frequently, we just waved and focused instead on mixing with other island neighbors we don't have the opportunity to socialize with as much. We chatted with the fellow who does our yard and with his charming wife, and we ran into the guy who had recently poured our new concrete driveway. I was glad we ran into him, because I wanted to compliment him on the great job he had done. Next, we bumped into our plumber, another of our old-house heroes.

As we worked the crowd, I came to understand the pattern of those in attendance. The invitees seemed to belong to one of four broad categories: full-time retired islanders with whom we routinely socialized; other full-time islanders who provided the services on which we all depended; another group of full-timers—basically, those who did not fit into either of my first two groupings but who frequented Robert's favorite bar on the island; and those involved, in one fashion or another, with Robert's farming enterprises. Most of this last group we didn't know, but they were easy to identify, because they were clumped together on the far side of the pool, engaged in earnest conversation, seemingly oblivious to the frivolity and merriment around them. As I watched, I noticed that several in this group appeared to be arguing in a "we'd better keep this quiet" sort of way. That and how they occasionally looked around, seemingly to ensure no one was listening, made me want to get closer and do just that.

As I stood, contemplating how best to make that move, however, the dinner bell—literally, a large bell hung near the food table—rang, and the party underwent an immediate transformation. That sound, followed quickly by Georgia's announcement that it was time to eat, caused most conversations to end, and people refocused their attention instead on how best to maneuver into whichever serving line promised to move most rapidly. While my opportunity for eavesdropping on the feuding farmers was missed, all was not lost, as I was able to take advantage of the thinning crowd around the bar and secure a new round of drinks.

As I returned with the refills, I found that Jill had finally settled into a conversation with several members of her card group. I recognized Roxy; Janice, the wife of my fishing buddy Kenny; Gigi, Janice's sister; and several others. I handed Jill a fresh beer and started looking for someone new to talk with, which didn't take long. I saw that Kenny looked to be in the same predicament. Kenny and I were able to get down quickly to important (at least to us) business—talking about how many fish he had caught that morning. I knew he and a friend had gone out in search of redfish, and I was anxious to learn how they'd done. I was also hopeful that, if they'd been successful, I might be able to get Kenny to tell me where they'd fished and, critically, what bait they'd used. I've learned over the years that the chances of pulling that information out of a good fisherman improves dramatically if you are standing near a bar with drinks in your hands. As it turned out, Kenny and his friend had enjoyed a very successful morning. He pulled his cell phone out to show me pictures that documented the triumph. One redfish was twenty-five inches long, and the other was just shy of the twenty-seven-inch limit. Those were some nice fish. As I enthused about his catch, I discreetly but deliberately maneuvered us nearer the bar, and once Kenny's glass emptied, I ordered up refills (a critical part of my information-gathering strategy). But just as he had begun to describe the specific area they'd fished, further conversation was effectively drowned out by the sound of a booming voice nearby.

It didn't take us long to identify the source of the interruption (truthfully, we both already suspected who the speaker would be)—a voice that despite being loud, managed at the same time to be almost unintelligible. This intrusive voice belonged—as we knew it would—to one of Robert's farming peers, a guy who owned one of the largest, most expensive houses in town, an imposing structure to which neither Kenny nor I had ever been invited. I had noticed him earlier quarreling with the other farmers, but now his voice didn't seem to be as unhappy. Rather, he appeared now to be enjoying himself—actually, to be enjoying himself a lot. From this I deduced that he probably had been to the bar several times more than either Kenny or I.

I had always wondered why this guy spoke the way he did. I'd theorized that he might have learned to speak like that on the farm (needing to yell at his field hands or something); however, none of the other farmers on the island spoke that way, so I'd grudgingly discarded that hypothesis. For a while, I'd theorized that he might have had a hearing issue, but I never saw any other evidence of that affliction, so I'd had to give up that explanation as well. My current, and admittedly favorite, hypothesis was that he just wanted to make sure everyone could hear what he was saying, whether they wanted to listen to him or not. Whatever the explanation, he frequently spoke in an exceptionally loud manner. And, I'd come to learn, the more booze he consumed, the louder his voice became.

This guy had always been somewhat of an enigma to me. I knew he was a successful farmer, and he was a good-looking fellow, in a tall, Burt Reynolds sort of way. I'd observed that some of the ladies in town seemed to think so as well. But the racket he made when he spoke was, to me at least, an annoyance. I tried to tolerate it, and eventually I had come to consider the speaker just another in the island's large cast of colorful characters. But I knew that, for some reason, Kenny really didn't like the guy. My friend chose this moment to confirm that antipathy with a concise summary of how he felt about the guy.

"Asshole!" Kenny mumbled.

I laughed and suggested we try to move to a less noisy location. We had just started to search out a spot where we could resume our fishing discussion when one of our mutual friends, a part-timer from Ohio named Rucker, stopped us to ask who the loudmouth was.

"That, my friend," Kenny responded, "is the island's biggest jerk!"

I quickly added, "Rucker, you can't mean to tell me you've never met Mr. R. V. Dodge?"

"Oh," exclaimed Rucker, "so that's R. V. Dodge. No, I've never met him, but I've heard a lot about him."

"Yep," Kenny said. "That's R. V. Dodge in all his glory. Did I mention he's also an asshole?"

We all laughed and moved to a location where we might be able to continue our conversation. We had just started to chat about how Rucker's trip from Ohio had gone when the band began to play. It was immediately obvious, given the band's level of amplification, that further dialogue would have to wait. We shrugged and turned to listen to the music.

As I had suspected, the band proved to be very good, and the lead singer—an attractive, blue jean–clad brunette who sang effortlessly in her bare feet, one of which was always tapping in time to the music—was great. Kenny took off to procure any lady who would agree to dance with him, while I waved good-bye to Rucker and went in search of Jill.

It took me a few moments to locate her, as she'd positioned herself in a relatively out-of-the-way spot over by the west side of the pool, a spot that promised to be a fine location from which to watch, and occasionally access, the dance floor. I joined her, gave her a wink, and got a quick kiss in return. We squeezed each other's hands and turned to see who was dancing. I had to chuckle when I saw Kenny was boogying down with none other than Robert's ninety-one-year-old mother. It promised to be a great evening.

And it was. During the band's first set, Jill and I danced together a half dozen times. Kenny even managed to get her to dance once with him. Truthfully, by the time the band took a break, we needed to rest as well. We also needed a drink. When I returned from the bar, I noticed Jill was talking happily with our electrician friend, Eddie.

I came up behind him and, in my best imitation of a jealous husband, accused him of hitting on my wife.

We all laughed.

Eddie went along with the ruse, replying, "Of course I was, Jim! Next to my wife, she's the best-looking lady here. But my old lady's six months pregnant."

"Yeah, I know," I replied. "That's what worries me!"

We laughed again. Eddie had just opened his mouth to respond when Jill interrupted. "Will you boys please quit? Eddie just stopped by to see if you wanted to go fishing with him in the morning."

"Of course," I replied. "Your boat or mine?"

"Neither," he said. "I'm looking for someone to go grouper fishing with several of us on Mack Emory's boat. You know him, don't you?"

"I think I've met him before somewhere. Isn't he a fertilizer salesman?" I asked.

"Yeah. That's him," Eddie said.

Jill quickly added, "Jim, we met him and his wife, Lois Anne, last Christmas at Tarpon Lodge when we were there for the Beacon of Hope benefit. Surely you remember chatting with them?"

"Actually," I said, hoping Jill would catch the humor in what I was attempting to convey, "I don't really recall talking with him, but I certainly do remember his wife."

"You would!" she replied. Then, without missing a beat, she came back with her own challenge, one I hoped was also delivered in jest, "Now that you mention it, I remember Mack was looking good himself!" She leaned backward with a look that managed to convey both glower and grin and waited for a comeback.

By this time, Eddie appeared to be unsure if we were serious. I noticed he had begun to shuffle his feet and look for a way to make a quick escape.

I winked at Jill. She stuck her tongue out at me. Wordlessly we'd agreed to let Eddie off the hook of our little flirtation. She hugged me, and I put my arm around her shoulder.

"Don't worry, Eddie," I said. "We're just kidding. But isn't it kind of late to be putting a trip together?"

"Actually," he replied, "we've had this trip planned for a while, but one of my buddies got arrested last night, and now, well, he's a little bit detained."

At that, we all laughed. "What'd he get arrested for?" I asked.

"Oh, you know, it was the usual thing—DUI. And he was operating with a suspended license. I think they're going to keep him for a while this time."

"Got ya," I replied. Then, getting back to the fishing invitation, I asked, "What kind of boat does Mack have?"

"He's got a thirty-two-foot Contender, with twin three hundred Yamahas. It'll fish six easily, and it's outfitted the way it should be."

"What's the weather going to be like? I don't have much of a stomach for swells."

Eddie replied, "That shouldn't be a problem. Wind's forecast at five to ten out of the east. Seas about two feet. Can't do much better than that."

"That sounds perfect. What time y'all leaving?" I asked.

"Six thirty in the morning. We're planning to leave from Mack's house on the west end of Emerald. You just drive up the street and park anywhere you can find a spot. We'll all be out back. So, you in, Jim?"

"You bet," I replied. "What do I need to bring?"

"Not a thing. I'm bringing a cooler full of beer and food. Mack already has all the rods rigged, and there'll be plenty of bait aboard."

"Damn, Eddie, sounds like fun. I'll be there. Thanks."

As he walked away, Jill said, "That was sure nice of him to think to include you."

"It was," I agreed. "Now I hope I won't make a fool out of myself by puking over the rail all day."

"Well, we'd better get you home and sober you up. You're going to need some sleep if we're going to prevent that from happening," she said.

"Yeah, I guess so." I hated to leave such a good party, but it's not every day I get invited to go grouper fishing.

We quickly found Georgia and Robert, explained why we had to leave, thanked them for including us, and walked to the car. Truthfully, by the time I chivalrously opened the car's door for Jill, I was already thinking about how delicious a fried grouper sandwich was going to taste for the next night's dinner.

Chapter Three

It was dark the next morning when I parked on the grass in front of what I hoped was the Emory residence. I checked my watch: six twenty on the dot. I'd made a point of arriving a little early, understanding as I did that there's not much worse in Saint James City's male world than being late for a fishing trip. Even so, I concluded from the number of cars already parked on the street and from the quiet voices coming from behind the house that I was likely one of the last to arrive. I made a note to myself to keep this in mind should I ever be invited to go grouper fishing with them again. As I walked around the corner of the house, I saw that the boat was already off its lift and moored to the dock. I noticed, too, that the vessel's rod holders were filled with expensive, heavy-duty rod and conventional reel combos; the boat's engines were silently idling; and the craft's running lights were casting colorful reflections on the lagoon's quiet water. I also noticed five guys, either lounging on the boat or impatiently leaning against pilings on the dock. It was clear all the preparations had been completed. No question about it: I was late.

"Good morning, guys," I said quietly as I moved into the glow of the dock's floodlights.

"Glad you made it, Jim," Eddie said. "We were beginning to worry maybe you'd overslept."

"Sorry," I said. "I got held up in traffic!" I was trying to defuse the tension with a little humor, understanding that everyone would recognize I likely had not encountered even a single vehicle on my short drive.

"Yeah," agreed the guy slouched behind the steering wheel against the leaning post. "Traffic *can* be rough this time of morning. I'm Mack. It's good to have you aboard."

"Thanks. I appreciate the invitation."

"Jim," Eddie said, "you know everyone else, don't you?"

I looked around and recognized our lawn guy, the pest-control guy, the guy who cleans our pool, and one of our favorite bartenders.

"Yeah, I do. How're y'all doing?"

They all mumbled something about being good.

With the necessary introductions out of the way, Mack said, "OK. Let's get going. We've got a long way to run before we can start catching fish."

I somewhat awkwardly climbed into the boat. Eddie and one of the other guys undid the lines that held the boat to the dock, then stepped aboard. I could tell from the practiced manner in which they performed these tasks that, unlike me, this was not their first trip out with Mack. I made another note to myself that I would be wise to pay attention to how they did things.

Mack calmly backed the boat away from the dock, gently shifted into forward, and began to idle smoothly toward the channel. I've learned that you can tell a lot about what kind of boater someone is just by watching how he or she handles the simple stuff. From the composed way Mack had gotten us going, I already felt good about his skills. I was pleased to note that he obeyed the slow speed requirements until we were past the resume speed markers, and I admired that he wasted no time in proficiently and easily bringing the boat onto plane, heading north up the channel. I'd wondered if we would go out into the gulf around the southern tip of Sanibel or through of one of the passes farther to the north. Now I knew the answer.

To me, there is something almost magical about the start of any boating trip. That sensation is especially strong whenever an expedition gets under way in the dark. There is just a feeling, an emotion almost, whenever I see the shimmer of moon and stars on the water, feel the glow from comforting marker beacons, watch the faint reflections from distant lights on shore, and feel the pull of ocean beyond the dark shadows of the land. I don't know if others feel that same sensation. I've never really asked anyone about it, but I suspect that most—well, at least most men—do. Why else would so many guys love getting out of their warm beds so early, so often, to go fishing? It's probably something instinctual in us all. Whatever the cause, that feeling was especially intense this morning, and I was already enjoying the trip.

I noticed that most of the others on the boat had by now found places to settle down on deck to take a nap. I was especially envious of Eddie and our yard guy, who had pulled beanbag chairs from a locker, placed them in the corners of the transom, and appeared to be comfortably snuggled into them in preparation of going to sleep. I was too excited to do that. Instead, I positioned myself alongside Mack and braced myself against the leaning post as he had done, with my knees slightly bent to absorb the shock of the boat as it landed against the water after clearing a swell. I could read on the GPS that the boat was running, seemingly effortlessly, at almost forty knots. I was impressed.

About ten minutes later, I noticed Mack ease the throttles back and steer the boat toward the west. I knew then that we were going to go out into the gulf through Redfish Pass, a deep strait that separates Captiva and North Captiva Islands. Although you'd never know it today, this passage didn't exist until the hurricane of 1921. Now, every time I go through this wide cut, I marvel at the strength of Mother Nature and consider the fragility and vulnerability of what humans create and value.

Mack slowed the boat to the required twenty-five miles per hour for this channel and, with precision, steered the boat through the pass and closely past the floating marker that indicated safe passage through the surrounding shoals. I was glad to notice that this was all clearly displayed on his GPS plotter. The captain then pointed the bow due west; accelerated to forty knots; and pushed a couple of buttons on the GPS, which locked the boat on to a heading for a spot marked on his electronic charts. I noted that the spot was labeled and numbered.

I asked Mack how far out we would be heading.

He replied, "About fifty miles." He pointed out the reading on his display, which showed "Distance to Mark." I saw that it read forty-nine point eight, and as I watched, I could see it was steadily decreasing. I made another note to myself to try not to ask any more stupid questions. As I studied the chart, I could see that the depth at the spot to which we were heading was shown as almost one hundred feet. I also noticed another reading on the display that was labeled "Time to Mark." This showed one hour and thirteen minutes. I complimented Mack on how well his boat was performing and asked him a couple of questions about the boat. I gathered from his responses that he wasn't much of a talker. That was OK, because neither am I. I turned my attention to watching the sea and the sky.

As Eddie had promised, the surface was smooth, almost glassy, but there were, in fact, still some significant swells. I supposed they were rolling in from some faraway Mexican storm. They didn't present a problem for us, but at the speed we were traveling, the boat occasionally would fly off the back of the larger waves and crash back into the water. I made sure to keep my knees bent and to keep one hand hanging on to the boat's T-top for support. Despite the boat's occasional impressive impacts, the trip really wasn't uncomfortable, so I was able to look around at the surrounding sea.

Soon the sun began to clear the eastern horizon, slowly rising to spread a diffused light over the gulf. This delicate glow was beautiful to behold as it reflected through a mist that seemed to caress the ocean's surface while floating over it. I may have seen impressions of violet and lavender, but those shades were so quickly transformed into something else by the intensifying rays of the sun that whether I had actually seen them was by no means a certainty. These mauve shadows quickly transitioned into an indigo tint, which impatiently faded toward an azure blush. Even as I marveled at what I had seen, that color vanished too, disappearing as if it had never even existed, replaced by what might have been, or might not have been, an emerald translucence. And then that, too, was gone, and it was daylight.

"Wow!" I exclaimed softly.

"That was pretty cool, huh?" Mack asked.

"You saw it, too?" I asked.

"Yeah. I think so." He laughed. "If you come out here when the sun's coming up, sometimes you'll see this. It's always hard to know exactly what it is you've seen, but one thing's for sure: it's something," Mack replied.

"I'll agree with you on that," I said. "That was pretty special."

With that shared experience, Mack became more conversational. He asked if I did much grouper fishing.

"When I was a kid, I used to go out on head boats with my dad. That was always fun. We used to catch a lot of fish, too," I replied.

Mack responded, "Not many of those boats around anymore, since most of the inshore reefs have been fished out. Now, to get a good catch, they have to make a two- or three-hour run in and out. And that's too time-consuming and expensive for most tourists."

"Yeah," I agreed. "That's a shame though. Those trips were always a lot of fun. Have you been doing this a long time?"

"A very long time!" Mack said with a grin. "I can remember going out with my grandfather when I was six. He had a nice wooden sportfisherman. It wasn't fast by today's standards, but it was a classic. I really loved that boat. Back then, we'd only have to go out fifteen or twenty miles, and we'd load the boat. And, of course, we didn't have to worry about catch limits. We'd catch as many as we thought we'd feel like cleaning when we got home."

"That's something," I replied. "I used to catch a lot of fish with my granddad and my dad, too. Mullet and trout, mostly. But that was still a lot of fun. And I know what you mean about keeping as many as you'd want to clean. Having to slap at sand gnats and mosquitoes while cleaning fish was always a consideration in that calculus. I guess that was one of nature's checks and balances."

Mack chuckled. "I guess, but we sure caught a lot of fish back then. Now you can't even keep enough to justify a trip. Not that I let that stop me, though."

"I understand that," I agreed. "Sometimes just getting out on the water's enough to justify it all."

"Yep. Hopefully, today won't be one of those days. I want to catch some fish."

"Me, too," I agreed. "I've always heard that the secret to catching grouper is knowing where to fish—knowing where the rocks are on the bottom. Is that how you fish?"

"You're right on," Mack said. "You can't just come out here and drop a hook in the water. You do that, and you'll be wasting your time. You've got to know where the structure on the bottom is. It's mostly sand out here, but there are some spots with rocks, wrecks, and coral heads, and that's where all the fish hang out. You drop your hook on that, and you'll catch fish. You drop it twenty feet away, and you'll catch nothing."

"Can you spot those on your charts?" I asked.

"Sometimes you can get in areas where the contour lines are tight, and that might work out. But that's not really the best way," Mack replied.

"So you pick up the spots on your sonar?"

"You always want to keep an eye on those things," Mack agreed. "You can never tell when you'll be running along and stumble across what looks like it could be the mother lode of grouper holes. If you're lucky enough to do that, you need to mark the spot on your electronics and come back to explore it. But that's unusual. Mostly we just run out to one of our numbers, spots we've had success on in the past."

"So having good numbers is important?" I asked.

Mack looked me in the eye, as if he were trying to determine the level of my IQ, and slowly smiled. "To a grouper fisherman, there's not much in the world more important than a good book of numbers. I'm serious when I say that. Over the years there have been a lot of fights, and a lot of people killed, too, over grouper numbers."

"I bet," I said. "I remember when I went out on head boats that the captains had thick black leather notebooks that they kept near the pilot wheel, frequently referred to, and occasionally wrote things in. Those books came aboard with the captain and left with the captain. I never saw the deckhands, or anyone else, look in those books."

"Nope," Mack agreed. "Back then, those books were sacred. Today, numbers are usually kept electronically, but they are still guarded just as closely. You might share some numbers with your best friend, but the whole book is probably passed along only when you are on your deathbed. A lot of times, its dispensation will even be specified in the captain's will, since it's one of the most valuable assets in his estate."

"Are those books ever sold?" I asked.

"Yeah, sure. But only when those old boys are really hard up, like maybe if they need a new boat or they're going through a divorce. But the buyer sure better beware."

"What do you mean?" I asked.

"Well, numbers look like numbers, if you know what I mean. I've heard stories of captains creating fake books when they needed to raise some quick cash."

We both laughed.

"Mack, if you don't mind me asking, how'd you get your numbers?"

"Like most people, a little from here, a little from there. I got my grandfather's book; my daddy gave me his book, although he really didn't do that much fishing. My buddies gave me some. But some of them are sites I discovered myself while I was out fishing. See some rocks on the depth finder, drop some bait down, and mark it if you bring up a fish. If you do that long enough and keep good records, you'll eventually have a decent book."

"I noticed on your chart that the spots you've marked have both names and numbers," I said.

"Yep."

"Is that a code or something?"

"Yep."

I could tell from Mack's last two answers that we had reverted to his previous style of communication. "You're not going to tell me what they mean, are you?"

"Nope. If you knew that, I'd have to kill you," Mack said, laughing.

Chapter Four

Ten minutes later, we were over the spot Mack had targeted. As the boat slowed, the other members of the crew had come alive. Minutes later, we were all fishing. Because there was little wind or current, Mack had elected to drift fish. Each line had been baited with either a live pinfish, a live squirrelfish, or with a chunk of cut mullet. Each angler was confidently extolling the merits of the particular type of bait he had selected or ridiculing the choices the others had made. I had gone with a small squirrelfish, simply because that was what had come up in the long-handled net I had dipped in the deep live well. I noticed most of the others had selected pinfish, but Eddie, whom I suspected was the most experienced fisherman of the bunch, had baited his hook with a sizable chunk of mullet.

I recognized the tackle that we were using was a common grouper rig, also known as a Florida Rig. A forged heavy-duty circle hook (required by federal and state law for all grouper fishing) was secured to a length of fluorocarbon leader material—a six-foot length of line that, from the feel of it, had to be at least eighty-pound test. That was, in turn, tied to a heavy-duty swivel. Above that was a short length of fluorocarbon, which had been threaded through a green plastic bead, a red plastic bead, an egg-shaped lead sinker, and then another set of matching beads. I knew the purpose of the beads was to cushion the swivel from the impact of the weight as it bounced off the bottom. Above that was tied a heavy-duty snap swivel, which in turn was snapped into a swivel tied to the main fishing line, which I guessed was probably a fifty-pound braid. That was all there was to it: a strong, basic arrangement that had been used for decades to pull grouper from rocks, reefs, and wrecks on the gulf's floor.

I remembered from previous grouper trips that the technique for fishing with this rig is simple. The baited hook is lowered until the lead weight comes in contact with the ocean floor. The fisherman then turns the handle of the reel just enough to lift the rig's weight off the bottom. Doing this allows the bait to move freely and permits the angler to feel the fish when it picks up the bait. Before the advent of the circle hook, which was introduced to reduce the incidence of gut hooking fish—an outcome often fatal to undersized fish—the necessary fishing technique, once you felt a nibble, had been to "set the hook" by aggressively yanking the rod upward. If you do this when fishing with a circle hook, you usually will pull the hook from the fish's mouth. The correct circle-hook technique is, as soon as you feel the fish's bite, to simply start to reel in the line. This action causes the fish to pull against the pressure, essentially causing it to hook itself in the rim of its mouth. Once you feel the fish begin to pull against you, it is critical to raise the rod tip and reel like crazy to try to keep the fish from entangling itself in the rocks. If that happens, your options are limited. You can release pressure on the line for a couple of minutes, and if you're lucky, the fish will think it is free and swim out of the rocks. But if you haven't been living right, you will eventually have to break off the line, a task that is not easy, given the heavy nature of the tackle.

As soon as I suspended my bait over the bottom, I felt a bump, reeled in on the line, and had a hookup. From the fight it put up, I thought this was likely a decent-sized fish—not huge, but probably a keeper. I was a little surprised that it fought against me all the way to the surface. My left arm had begun to burn from the strain by the time I finally, through the gulf's blue translucence, had my first glimpse of the fish. What I had brought up was not a grouper, but instead a very nice red snapper. I was a little disappointed since I had been looking so forward to catching a grouper, but my associates on the boat had a different view. To them, this was an even better catch. I wasn't really convinced until they reminded me that you would pay a higher price per pound in the fish market for red snapper than you would for grouper. With that, I didn't feel as bad, and, besides, I had the honor of having caught the first fish of the day. Bragging rights are always good.

Eddie was the next to hook up, and from the fight he had on his hands, it was clear he had a much bigger fish. For a few minutes, he had a struggle on his hands and had to put his all into the fight, as evidenced by lots of grunting, yelling, and cursing as he pulled, reeled, and fought against his adversary. We were all focused on what he was going to bring up. Finally, when we could see the flash of the fish thirty feet or so below the surface, we could tell he had hooked on to a sizable black grouper. When the fish finally neared the surface, Mack brought out a large-mouth, long-handled catch net and held it over the water near where he estimated the fish would likely emerge. When the fish eventually came up, Eddie expertly kept it in position, and Mack quickly encircled it from the rear in the net's folds of enveloping green mesh. The fish was then lifted on board. The catch then, despite the fish's last desperate flopping to somehow, against all odds, secure its freedom, was complete. The grouper was so large it didn't have to be measured and quickly was placed in the boat's ice locker.

As soon as the fish had come over the gunwale, all the other fishermen on board whooped loud congratulations to Eddie.

He nimbly replied, "Guess that cut mullet worked out OK, huh?"

Several of us grumbled, while Jim, the bartender, opined that Eddie had just gotten lucky.

For the next hour or so, we all caught fish. Red snapper seemed to prefer my squirrelfish offering, while grouper seemed to fancy the tenders of mullet and pinfish about equally. Eventually, the bites stopped, and Mack decided we had drifted off the rocks. We all reeled in and took a break as he repositioned the boat.

As we moved to our new location, I took time to look at the tackle on all Mack's rods. I was expecting to see that each was rigged a little bit differently, because that's the way my outfits always seem to end up. How I rig my stuff depends largely on whatever I happen to have handy in my tackle bag at the particular moment when I need to rerig. I was surprised Mack's rods were not rigged like that; instead, they were all rigged absolutely identically: matching hooks, lines, green and red beads, leads, and swivels. I was impressed. I guessed he must have been a little obsessive or something.

After another drift over the rocks, we were near our boat's aggregate limit for grouper. Because I was the only one to have caught snapper, we still had room for a few fish under that restriction. We'd just decided to take a break before repositioning the boat and to try some of the cold fried chicken Eddie had supplied for lunch when we noticed a boat approaching from the east. I wasn't really surprised that we would have company, but I was certainly disappointed that we might have to share our slice of productive fishing with someone else. Unfortunately, the captain of the approaching vessel seemed to want to occupy our exact location. I had to shake my head—no other boats as far as the eye could see, and this guy wants our precise spot. I wasn't familiar with grouper-fishing protocol, but I had to guess he wasn't demonstrating the best angling etiquette.

The other boat continued to approach, and by the time we had finished our chicken, it was idling straight toward us. There were four men on board. The boat was larger than ours. Three three-hundred horsepower Mercury engines hung off the stern. It was, without question, a beautiful and expensive craft. I didn't recognize it, but I could tell several of the others must have, because I could hear them mumbling their views about its owner.

"Asshole!" was Eddie's considered opinion. "Dickhead!" was Jim's concise judgment, while Big Mike, our normally affable yard guy, labeled the new arrival with a more subdued, but still heartfelt, "Son of a bitch!" Mack, I noticed, remained silent.

The approaching boat coasted within twenty feet before its captain addressed ours in an irritatingly loud voice—so much for continuing to enjoy a quiet day on the water. By that time, of course, I, too, knew who the captain was. It was none other than the inebriated farmer from the night before, R. V. Dodge. I also recognized his passengers, members of the group I had seen arguing last night around the side of the pool.

In his booming voice, R. V. enthused, "Mack, how the hell are you?"

Our captain, to his credit, replied in a quieter manner, demonstrating, I thought, a decibel level far more appropriate for a conversation taking place over a distance of only a few feet, "I'm fine, R. V."

I was amused, and pleased to note, that Mack left the conversation with that, clearly placing the responsibility for continuing the discussion on R. V.

But R. V. didn't miss a beat. "Well, that's good! Y'all catch any fish out here?"

"No. We haven't done any good at all. In fact, we were just getting ready to move and look for a better spot."

I had to admire the dexterity with which Mack had cleanly perjured himself. I conjectured this might have been a skill set he'd cultivated during his years as a fertilizer salesman.

"Damn!" responded R. V. "It's a shame when you burn up a hundred gallons of fuel to go fishing, bring a bunch of buddies with you to show off to, and don't catch nothing. I had hopes for this spot, too. I'd heard it was a good one."

"Where'd you hear that from, R. V?" asked Mack.

"Oh, a really, really good friend of mine gave me a book of numbers last week. Told me all of them were good spots, too. You got this location in your book, Mack?"

"Nah. We just stopped when I thought I saw something on the bottom that looked promising. But I guess it must have just been a false echo. We're going to take off to another spot. I wouldn't waste any of your time here, if I were you," replied Mack.

"I hear you," said R. V. "But, since we've come so far, I think we'll try it for a while anyway."

"Hope it works out for you, R. V." Mack looked at us in the stern of his boat and said, "You guys back there, hang on. We're going to take a little ride."

With that he slammed the twin throttles down and spun the boat's steering wheel toward the south. The result of these actions was to send a sizable wake directly toward the side of R. V.'s vessel. As I looked back, I could see it rocking from gunwale to gunwale, with the passengers holding on to keep from being tossed overboard. I was a little amused at this lack of manners on Mack's part. He must have been a little bit angry, I surmised, that R. V. had somehow gotten his hands on at least one of his good numbers.

Mack kept the boat on a forty-knot plane to the south more than long enough for R. V.'s boat to disappear below the horizon. Then I saw him look at his GPS and apparently select a new fishing location. With the push of a button, he locked the boat's autopilot on to this new destination, and the boat gently turned to the east and headed toward the selected spot.

As the boat settled on to its new course, I studied Mack's face. I thought I could tell from the set of his jaw and the squint around his eyes that he was still upset. After a few minutes, I decided to engage him in conversation—just to see if that might help to calm him down.

"It's a shame R. V. has that number," I said. "That sure seemed like a good fishing spot."

For a long moment, Mack seemed to ignore me. Then he slowly turned and looked deeply into my eyes, as if trying to decide if it was even worth his time to respond to my inane observation. He must have concluded that not doing so would have been rude.

"Yeah. It *was* a very good spot—one of my best. I'm totally pissed off that that idiot now has it in his book. Knowing him, he'll fish it out and ruin it in no time."

"Don't others have it in their books?" I inquired.

"Well, obviously, someone must have," he said. "But that surprises me, because I've never seen anyone else fishing there. I just stumbled on it a couple of years ago when I was drift fishing. I've always thought of it as my own secret location, a spot I could always catch fish on when all else failed. I'm going to have to take it out of my book now. Bastard!"

Chapter Five

The next week flew past. Jill and I had jointly decided that it was time for us to devote some energy to maintaining our property. My project was to thin out the areca palms that surrounded our pool enclosure. This tropical tree, sometimes called a butterfly palm, is quite attractive with its slender pinnate leaves. While it is frequently planted indoors as a patio palm, it is also often planted outdoors as a privacy screen. Its clustering trunks, if left untrimmed, will produce a nearly impenetrable wall of densely clustered leaves; that is exactly what had happened around our pool cage. Initially, we had liked the privacy provided by the plants. But, eventually, we had come to realize that we needed to decide which we enjoyed more: privacy or being able to feel a cooling breath of fresh air on a hot summer afternoon. We opted for the breeze.

Jill, for her part, had elected to take on the task of cleaning a seemingly always festering layer of mold and mildew from the white, painted wooden decks and stairs that surround our house.

In Southwest Florida, this is a never totally completed chore, necessitated by the region's ubiquitous heat and humidity. Effectively dealing with this scourge of nature requires two things: a pump sprayer to provide a heavy application of bleach and a good pressure washer to scour it all away. This task is one Jill enjoys performing. Over the years that we've been married, I've come to appreciate that there is something in her DNA that necessitates that any soiled surface, even if it's only moderately grubby, be attacked as quickly and as aggressively as possible to return it to a nearly sterile condition. Consequently, she actually enjoys blowing away the greenish tinges that seem to be constantly emerging on our woodwork.

It took most of the week for me to thin the palms. I found that there was really no easy or quick way to do it. What I eventually concluded worked best was for me to get down on my knees and use a hand-pruning saw to cut through whichever of a tree's multiple trunks didn't satisfy my finely tuned sense of a trunk being where a trunk should be. This, I soon learned, while being the most satisfying portion of the task, was not the most difficult. The hardest part of the job, I painfully discovered, was bending over to cut the felled trunks into three-foot sections, as required by our trash-pickup regulations. All the resulting debris had to be arranged in bundles and tied securely in place with baling twine. And then, of course, each bundle had to be dragged or carried to the street for pickup. By the end of the week, I was exhausted. Not only was I tired, I was also more than a little disappointed that needing to complete this job had caused me to turn down a midweek invitation from my friends Rucker and Kenny to join them on a grouper-fishing expedition, an outing that I subsequently heard had been very successful—so successful, in fact, that they had decided to host a Saturday evening fish fry at Kenny's house. There are a lot of pleasant activities in Saint James City, but few of them are more fun than attending fish fries. Jill and I both were looking forward to the party.

***

"Kenny," I said, "you guys must have had a good trip."

"We damn sure did," Kenny answered. "Not only did we limit out on grouper, but we caught a cooler full of grunts and snapper, too. I wish you could have been with us."

"I wish I could have been, too. Maybe next time. Y'all going again anytime soon?"

"Probably midweek. I'll try to make sure Rucker saves you a spot on his boat."

"Thanks, Kenny. I appreciate it. Now, what else has been going on?"

"I assume you've heard about R. V. Dodge's latest escapade?" Kenny asked.

"No. I haven't heard anything. What did he do now?"

"Well, from what I heard down at the bar, he got into a hell of a squabble with his neighbor," Kenny replied.

"Which one? The lady who lives west of him? Or the doctor?

"The lady. You know, she's an environmental activist. Apparently she and R. V. have had issues in the past, but this time he may have gone too far."

"All right, Kenny, what'd he do now?"

"Well, this lady owns the lots that sit behind R. V.'s house. She bought them a couple of years ago because of the bald eagles that nest in the lots' Australian pines. The birds have been nesting there for years. Every winter, they fly back, rebuild their nest, lay a couple of eggs, and raise the fledglings. She's now turned the lots into a private sanctuary for the eagles. You know how most people in town love those birds. Well, apparently, R. V. might not share that same sentiment. The way I heard the story, he'd acquired a high-priced drone and wanted to learn how to operate it. Anyway, he takes the new machine out on his back deck, and apparently, it didn't take him long to get the hang of it. The next thing you know, the environmentalist spots a drone near her eagles' nest. And, according to what she reported to the sheriff's department, someone was using the drone to harass the eagles, trying to drive them off their nest. Once she'd called the sheriff's office, she went to find out who was responsible. I imagine she suspected it was R. V. all along. Well, the way I heard the story, when she saw him operating that thing, she went absolutely ballistic. She stormed on to his deck, punched R. V. square in the face, grabbed the controller out of his hands, and stomped on it until there was nothing left but a pile of smoking wires and plastic!"

"Wow. I wish I'd been there to see that! What happened then?" I asked.

"The way it was explained to me," Kenny said "they started to yell at each other, with R. V. threatening to have her arrested for trespass and battery, and her threatening to have him prosecuted on federal charges of harassing a protected species. About that time, R. V.'s wife came outside, and once she found out what he'd done, she started whacking him, too. Apparently, by the time the sheriff's deputies arrived, they were both chasing him around the porch. Eventually, the deputies were able to get everybody calmed down, but they did arrest R. V., put him in a car, and took him off to jail, probably as much for his own protection as for anything else."

"Is he still there?" I asked Kenny.

"No. His lawyer quickly got him out on bail, but both he and the neighbor lady now have restraining orders against each other. I guess it'll all play out in court eventually."

"Kenny, you said they'd had issues in the past. What was that about?"

He laughed and said, "I'll tell you about that some other time, but right now, I've got to get me a drink and go cook some fish. Can I get you one?"

"Of course!" I replied.

Armed with refreshment, I started to circulate through the crowd of mostly friends and neighbors. I'd managed to shake hands or speak with about half of them when I heard Kenny's wife announce that dinner was served. I was hungry and looking forward to it.

Jill, along with most of the other ladies in attendance, had brought a side dish for the gathering. Her contribution was a large Crock-Pot of her famous cheese grits, grits so good that even Yankees will eat them. Another had brought baked beans. Someone else had made coleslaw. A potato salad, a baked corn casserole, a pasta salad, a delicious tossed salad, and a tray of hot fragrant corn bread completed the buffet offerings. The appetizer selections had long since disappeared, and I had made a note to ask Jill to try to get the recipe for the baked jalapeño poppers

I had enjoyed. A nearby dessert table, highlighted by several homemade key lime pies, promised postdining bliss. But the highlight of the meal was, without question, the four aluminum baking pans full of freshly fried fish. I was thankful Kenny had thoughtfully labeled each pan: grouper, snapper, redfish, and shark. I quickly found a place in line, and I'm not ashamed to admit that, after I finished my first plate of food, I returned for another round. We may not have been in heaven, but in my opinion, we were close.

After everyone had all they cared to eat and drink, the party began to slowly to wind down. Most had found a comfortable place to sit and chat with friends, while savoring their last drinks. Eventually, as their glasses ran dry, the guests began to say their good-byes and leave to enjoy a night of repose. Jill and I, despite being close to falling into food-induced comas ourselves, stayed long enough to help Kenny and Janice clean up.

I gave Kenny a hand as he strained the cooled cooking oil from his deep fryer. We lined a large funnel with a conical coffee filter, slowly poured the used peanut oil into that, and let it drip back into the gallon jug in which it had come from the store. No sense in wasting good cooking oil—as long as you take care not to burn it and you carefully strain it clean of impurities, it can be reused several times. As we were waiting for the oil to slowly work its way through the filter, I asked Kenny again about the other times that R. V. and his neighbor had quarreled.

"Jim, I'm too drunk to tell you about it now, but if you want to go fishing in the morning, I'll do better than tell you about it; I'll *show* you what they were fighting over. You want to go?"

"Sure. What time?" I asked.

"I'll pick you up about eight o'clock at your dock. You want to pick up some shrimp?"

"I'll do it, and I'll be waiting on you."

By ten o'clock, the cleanup was complete, and we headed for home. It had been another great night in Saint James City.

Chapter Six

By seven fifty-five the next morning, I was sitting in an Adiron-
dack chair on my dock, newly purchased shrimp swimming in a
bucket by my side, two of my favorite light-duty rods prepped for
a day of inshore fishing, and my canvas tackle bag sitting by my
feet. A minute or so later, I heard the piercing squeal of ungreased
boat-lift bearings, a sound all too common in Saint James City,
echo down the canal from the direction of Kenny's house. I looked
that way and could see his boat moving silently toward the water. I
smiled to myself, knowing I'd be able to rib Kenny about the noise
he'd just created.

Five minutes later, he carefully eased the bow of his deck boat
against my dock and grabbed a piling to keep it from drifting
away. I passed the bucket of shrimp to him and stepped aboard
with my rods and bag. Kenny poured the shrimp into his bait
well, and I secured my gear. As soon as that was done, I gently
pushed the bow away from the dock toward the middle of the
canal. Kenny tossed the now-empty bucket onto the dock, put the

engine in gear, applied just enough power to move the boat at a speed sufficient to maintain steerage, and turned the craft's steering wheel in the direction we wanted to head.

"Morning, Jim!" Kenny cheerfully welcomed me.

Truthfully, given the condition I'd last seen him in, I was more than a little impressed with the joviality of his greeting.

"Good morning, Kenny!" I replied. "Glad to see you in such good spirits."

"Why in the heck wouldn't anyone be in good spirits on a glorious morning like this?" he retorted.

"Good point, Kenny. Good point. But I was afraid you might have found the noise from the bearings of your lift a mite painful this morning, given how much we all had to drink last night."

"Speak for yourself, Jim, but personally, I didn't imbibe all that heavily."

"Could have fooled me," I replied. "Now about that noise, when was the last time you greased those damn bearings?"

"I know you won't believe me, but it couldn't have been more than a month ago—at least, not more than six weeks ago."

"How about six *months* ago?" I kidded Kenny. "I hope that squealing didn't wake Janice."

"Me, too," agreed Kenny. "She was still in bed, sound asleep, when I left the house. I think, in fact, she may actually have been hurting a little bit from last night. When I get back, I'm going to regrease those bearings before I even go inside. Those damn things really were loud."

"That sounds like a great idea. Now where are we going?"

"Well, last night you were asking about the other times R. V. had run-ins with his environmentally passionate neighbor, so I thought I'd just show you where it all went down."

"Sounds good! Is it far from here?"

"No, it's just around on the bay. We'll be there in less than ten minutes. Then, after we see that, we can go fishing."

"Sounds like a plan."

***

"You see the second house from the right?" Kenny asked.

"The yellow one with the captain's walk?" I asked.

"Yeah, that's it. What do you see in front of it, down by the shore?"

"Not much," I replied. "Just a line of what look like small mangroves."

"A year ago, where you see those bushes today, you would have been looking at a beautiful stand of tall red mangroves, trees that had probably been in that spot for forty or fifty years."

"Uh-oh," I murmured. "Aren't those protected by law?"

Kenny started to laugh. "Yeah! They sure are. That's why I wanted you to see this."

"All right, so tell me what happened to them," I said.

He started to laugh again, obviously enjoying reflecting on what had transpired. I couldn't help myself from starting to chuckle along with him. Finally, I couldn't stand it any longer. I held up my hands, shaking them for emphasis, and said, "Darn it. What happened to those mangroves?"

"I'm sorry," he said, "I just can't help myself. Give me a minute, and I'll tell you."

He looked toward the open bay; took a deep breath, seemingly in an effort to control himself; exhaled loudly; then turned once again to look at me.

"When R. V. and his wife bought this place, those trees were tall, thick, and healthy. But they were most definitely blocking R. V.'s view of the open bay, a view that R. V. reasoned he'd just paid a million dollars to enjoy."

"You're not going to tell me he cut those trees down, are you?"

"Yep. In the best tradition of Hendry County agriculture, R. V. brought in a truckload of his best migrants and told them to 'get rid of them damn bushes,' so he and his wife could see the water! Well, those workers quickly got down to business, happy to enjoy a day's labor away from the tomato fields, cheerfully chopping away at some of San Carlos Bay's finest specimens of safeguarded mangroves. They had cut down half of those trees before the neighbors even knew what was going on. The same lady I told you about last night ran screaming to where they were working, where R. V. was keeping an eye on progress. She was, of course, soon screaming in R. V.'s face, demanding he stop the destruction. According to what I've been told, he did his best to ignore her, while encouraging his confused employees to keep chopping."

By this time I was laughing, too, unable to believe what I was hearing. "So what happened then?"

"Well, by the time the sheriff's deputies arrived, all the trees had been cut down, and his workers were happily loading the leftovers into a trailer. R. V., for his part, was sitting on his front porch sipping a scotch and water, and savoring his uninterrupted view of Sanibel Island. The way I heard it, when the deputies asked him for his version of what had happened, R. V. explained that he had just asked his workers to trim the trees back a little. But, since they didn't speak English all that well, they had apparently misinterpreted what he'd wanted done and had chopped them all the way to the ground. When the deputies asked him if he knew mangroves were a protected species and if he had a permit that allowed him to trim these trees, he acted surprised, saying that was the first he'd ever heard of needing permission to trim bushes in your own yard. The deputies apparently didn't agree with R. V.'s assessment and immediately wrote him a citation."

"Damn! So what happened after that?" I asked.

"Well, R. V., apparently being used to how justice is typically administered in Hendry County, wasn't overly concerned by the citation, figuring how much trouble could he possibly be in for simply chopping down some scraggly shrubs in his yard? He showed up at court on the day directed. From what I've been told, he might have already enjoyed several Bloody Marys with the eggs Benedict he'd had for breakfast, and when called in front of the judge, he began to offer, in his usual drawling slur, a noisy opinion about how ridiculous he thought the charges were that had been levied against him. He began to explain how he thought he was being harassed for essentially doing nothing more than cleaning up some nuisance weeds on his property, weeds that were interfering with his expensive view of San Carlos Bay.

"The judge listened to this for about fifteen seconds, before interrupting R. V. to ask if he was represented by counsel. R. V., indignant at being interrupted and starting to get hot under the collar, replied loudly that he 'didn't need a goddamned lawyer just because he'd cut down some ugly damn bushes!' The judge calmly responded to this by asking R. V. if he was aware of the potential penalties associated with the charges that had been levied against him.

"R. V., hoping to impress the judge with disdain for the court's penny-ante fines (he probably assumed they would be no more than a few hundred dollars), said, 'Your honor, I can save us all a lot of time and get us both to the bar a lot earlier today, if you'll just let me pay whatever the fine for this silly charge is going to be.'

"To which the judge replied, 'Mr. Dodge, I appreciate your concern with saving my time, and with your offer to take care of this matter expeditiously. To be clear, you have been charged with violation of the State of Florida's *1966 Mangrove Trimming and Preservation Act.* This act is intended to protect and preserve the state's valuable threatened mangrove resources from unregulated removal, defoliation, or destruction. It allows for permitted trimming of these trees, and in some cases, limited removal to preserve property owners' riparian rights. However, if said permitting is not secured, and/or if these trees are damaged, the person responsible for such will be liable for performing restoration by replanting said trees in the same location as each mangrove that was destroyed. According to the statute, such restoration will ensure that within a five-year period, a canopy equivalent to the area destroyed will be created. Where such is not practical, the damage may be offset by donating a sufficient amount of money to offset the impacts caused by the damage. In the case in question, this dollar amount of the required offset has been calculated at forty thousand dollars. In addition, a penalty of up to two hundred and fifty dollars per tree damaged may be levied. In this case, since there were a hundred and seven trees totally destroyed, this penalty would be twenty-six thousand, seven hundred and fifty dollars. Further, this act does not limit local government from enforcing additional penalties and provisions under its own authority. The local authority in this particular case is Lee County, and I have been notified that it is seeking in this case an additional forty-thousand-dollar penalty. The total amount of these charges is one hundred six thousand, seven hundred and fifty dollars. As I said before, I do appreciate your generous offer to expeditiously settle these charges, and since you have indicated that you are prepared to settle these charges today, I will direct you now to the clerk of the court to make the required payments.'

"Hearing this, R. V. replied in a markedly quieter voice, 'Your honor, perhaps I was a little hasty. I think I'd better find a lawyer.' The judge, an obvious twinkle in his eye, responded, 'Mr. Dodge, I think that would probably be in your interest. I will reschedule this hearing for one month from today.'"

"So, Kenny," I asked, "has this gone to trial?"

"Oh, yeah. And, from what I've been told, R. V. ended up paying forty thousand dollars in total penalties, plus the cost of having the trees replanted. Those trees on the shore are the ones he had to plant to replace what he cut down. He also had to pay court costs and attorney's fees. Altogether, this episode cost him a little over fifty thousand dollars."

"Damn!" I said. "That's a lot of money. But last night you said there were two things he'd done. What else did he do to get in trouble?"

"See that berm to the right of R. V.'s house? You can't really see it from here, but that bank goes around a retention pond. The purpose of the pond is, of course, to capture and cleanse any run-off from the neighborhood's streets before it flows into the bay.

Apparently, it was a county requirement that the pond be put in place before it would issue a permit to the developer. Well, apparently, R. V. didn't particularly care for having a pond of stagnant water next to his new million-dollar house, so he decided he'd just drain it into a ditch that runs into the bay. This time, though, he waited until his sensitive neighbor had gone north. Then he brought in his crew from the farm, along with some equipment, and had them jet a two-inch pipe through the back wall of the berm. I assume he figured no one would ever notice if there was actually no water in the pond. And he got away with it for a while. But, eventually, after she'd returned, a strong storm front had come through, and the neighbor noticed more water flowing through the ditch, and into the bay, than she thought there should be. Of course, once she saw what had been done, it didn't take her long to call the sheriff's department again. This time, since R. V. was a repeat offender, he had to fork out another fifty thousand dollars. And, now, of course, he's on probation. There's no telling what the eagle episode is going to cost him!"

"Kenny, I can't believe that guy! How stupid can you be? Doesn't he care about how much this is costing him?"

"Nah. R. V. couldn't care less. I've heard him say he netted almost three million dollars last year on tomatoes and watermelons. I think he sees these fines as just something else he can brag about with the boys at the bar."

"Jeez! I had no idea he made that much money farming. But, still, he can't like living next door to that neighbor. It doesn't sound like a happy neighborhood to me!"

"I don't think the neighbors will be having a block party anytime soon!"

"I reckon not," I agreed, "unless R. V. decides to move."

"Yeah," Kenny answered. "Or decides to die."

"Yeah, that might do it all right!" I laughed. "If that were to happen, I suspect the neighbors would have a party to remember."

"I'd damn sure want to be there," Kenny said.

"You really don't like R. V., do you?" I asked.

"Not a bit. He's an asshole."

Chapter Seven

"Some adjustment is required."

That's what I always tell folks when they ask how I'm enjoying retirement, and I mean it. Once you retire, in some ways, you've got to reinvent yourself. In my particular case, I'd enjoyed an almost forty-year career as a banker. In the latter stages of that career, I had risen to positions in which I enjoyed, at least in the world of finance, a fair measure of stature and respect. And, in many ways, my self-image, and to some extent my identity, had been built around this. But once I left the working world, that part of who I had been totally disappeared. So yes, some adjustment had been necessary.

The clothes I had hanging in my closet were one of the first things that had to change. As a banker, I'd always made a point of wearing professional-looking suits, white or blue shirts adorned with tasteful ties, and, of course, neatly polished black business shoes. An early boss had explained that, as a banker, it was important to convey an image that made depositors feel comfortable that they'd left their money with us—especially since you didn't really have their money any longer, having loaned most of it out to borrowers. But on Pine Island, all that banker attire was completely out of place. Worn canvas shorts, vented cotton fishing shirts, scuffed salt-stained boat shoes, and polarized Costa sunglasses had quickly become my new uniform. Once we'd moved to the island, it was clear I was no longer a banker. Now, instead of getting up and going to work every day, I was going fishing. At least, I was going fishing on days when the weather allowed. And when it didn't, there was always the tackle store or the bar. Yes, in retirement, some adjustment had been required.

And adjustment had been required for my wife as well. Of course, she'd had her own career. But beyond that, she'd also enjoyed (at least, I think she'd enjoyed) being married to a successful banking executive. Over the years, we'd gone together to countless conferences and conventions. And together, over many decades, we'd entertained thousands of clients. For years, that had been our life. In doing this, we'd met many interesting and intelligent people. We'd dined in some of the world's best restaurants, and we'd traveled much of the world—it had been a life we'd very much enjoyed.

And one part of that life I'd always particularly enjoyed was having Jill by my side. Not only is she a great life partner and adviser, she is also my best friend. We've always made a good team. And while it may not be politically correct to admit this, I've always loved just how attractive she is to look at. I've suspected, or at least I've hoped, that Jill, although she'd never admit to this, was pleased I found her so appealing. One aspect of our professional lives together that I think she most enjoyed was the opportunities it gave her to dress nicely. And I like to think that part of the pleasure she took from doing this was being able to dress for my enjoyment. But once we retired to Pine Island, the opportunities for her to continue doing that largely disappeared. I mean, there are only so many things you can do to dress up the short-sleeved cotton blouse and shorts you're going to wear to Woody's, one of Saint James City's few waterside bars. So, yes, she, too, had had some adjustments to make.

Fortunately, after a few months on the island, she'd been invited to participate in a card group to which several of her female acquaintances belonged. This group consisted of seven other women, all full-time island residents. Some of the girls in the group were married; some were not. But they all shared the following attributes: they were about the same age, they were attractive, they liked to occasionally dress nicely, they were fantastic cooks, and they enjoyed drinking quality wine. Playing cards (canasta, in particular) was the ostensible rationale for the existence of this group, but after about a year, their card-playing had become less and less frequent, and eventually this activity was replaced entirely by an even more intensive focus on food and wine. A weekly gathering of this nature in a quiet fishing village at the end of the road helped to fill Jill's need (and I think the needs of the other ladies) to occasionally wear something other than fishing clothes.

This group gets together every Tuesday evening at six o'clock. They rotate meeting at each member's home, with the lady whose turn it is to host responsible for providing the gourmet meal and appropriate accompanying beverages.

As you might expect, another activity that routinely takes place at these meetings is the exchange of island news, or as some might describe it, gossip. And, of course, while I would never gossip myself, I do always look forward to Jill returning from "cards," knowing she will probably have some interesting information about whatever activity might have recently been taking place on the island. I was not to be disappointed tonight.

"Hey, babe!" I said as I heard Jill come through the kitchen door from the second-floor deck. "How was the party?"

Truthfully, I already pretty much knew what the answer was likely to be, given the time she'd come home: nine thirty. That was about the average time of adjournment for this group, so I suspected the party had been a good one. If she'd come home earlier, the gathering would have been a dud; if she'd come home later, the party would have been great, and a lot more wine would have been consumed.

"It was good, baby! I'll tell you about it after I go upstairs and change clothes. How are the dogs?"

"They're good."

"I'll be back in a minute."

"Hurry back, baby."

She came back downstairs shortly. She'd exchanged her party clothes for more comfortable black leggings and a long-sleeved, gray knit shirt—her normal evening attire. She grabbed an Ultra 55 from the refrigerator and sat in her usual spot on the sofa. She assumed her normal position with her right leg pulled up under her. The other one was bent with the knee propped against the arm of the couch. Once she was settled comfortably, I began my friendly interrogation.

"What'd y'all have to eat?" I asked.

"Roxie fixed broiled jumbo shrimp served with spaghetti squash and topped with a delicious vodka-infused tomato and basil pasta sauce. I loved it. But you're not going to believe what I heard tonight!"

I knew she was dying to tell me something that was probably going to be especially juicy, but for some devilish reason, I wanted to make her fret about not being able to tell me about it for as long as possible. So I interrupted her, just for the fun of it.

"Where'd she get the fresh shrimp?" I asked.

"Oh, she always goes down to the fish house and gets the boys there to clean and devein them for her. And, of course, she always cooks them perfectly. They are never overcooked. But let me tell you—"

"No, wait," I interrupted. "Before you get into that, what else did y'all have to eat?"

"Well, she made each of us our own unique fresh shellfish and tropical fruit cocktails. Mine had mango medallions and star-fruit slices paired with shrimp and bronzed bay scallops. It was to die for. Now, what I—"

"Did you have wine?" I butted in, asking in what I hoped was an innocent manner.

"Jim, don't be stupid! Of course we had wine. We had a nice sauvignon blanc with the appetizer and a delightful Argentinean Malbec with the entrée. And for dessert—well, we didn't actually have dessert—we sipped a lovely eighteen-year-old Flor de Caña rum."

"You sipped it?"

"Well, some of us sipped it. Others might have drunk it a little bit more enthusiastically. It was really, really good. You need to buy us some. Now, let me tell—"

"You won't have to twist my arm to do that," I exclaimed, again stopping her in midsentence. "You know how I feel about Flor de Caña."

"Jim, damn it, if you interrupt me one more time, I'm never going to tell you what I heard tonight. And I know you want to hear it as badly as I want to tell you. So shut your mouth, so I can tell you what I heard."

"Oh, did you have something you wanted to tell me?" I answered as innocently as possible.

In response, she just glared. I knew then that I'd taken the fun too far and that it would be in my best interest to retreat a step or two. In other words, now I knew I was going to have to beg a little to get her to tell me what she'd heard.

"Oh, I'm sorry, baby. I was just pulling your leg. What did you hear?"

"Oh, it doesn't matter," she said. "It was nothing you'd want to hear about anyway."

"Of course I want to hear about it. Now what did you hear?"

"Oh, it was really nothing."

"Come on, baby. Please tell me. What did you hear?"

"Well, OK. I actually heard two things tonight, and one of them you're not going to believe. But, to start, did you hear about what happened to Kenny down at Froggy's?"

"No. I haven't heard a thing. What'd he get himself into down there this time?"

"Well," she began, "he almost got in a fight in the bar with R. V. Dodge last week."

"Kenny? I've never heard of him getting mad at anybody. What the hell happened?"

"According to Janice, he was sitting at the bar like he always does, just shooting the breeze with Steve Fairchild, when R. V. came in. Kenny waved a welcome to him and went back to the conversation he was enjoying with his friend. There weren't any empty stools, so R. V. stood near the end of the bar and started talking with Georgia's husband, Robert. Janice said Kenny had told her that R. V. looked drunk when he came in. Anyway, R. V. and Robert talked for a few minutes. Then R. V. called over Sarah, the lady who owns the bar, and in his loudest voice told her, 'Sarah, my dear, I want to buy everybody in this whole bar a drink.' Then in an even louder, and even more obnoxious, voice he added, 'Everybody, that is, except for Kenny!'"

"Uh-oh!" I said. "I don't think he should have done that. What'd Kenny do?"

"Well, Janice said he kept his cool and just asked R. V. why he wasn't going to buy him a drink. R. V. said, "Cause I figure if you don't have a drink in your hand, then there'll be no reason for you to keep sitting on that damn stool and no reason for me to not be able to sit on it.' Then he laughed.

"Kenny, bless his soul, didn't reply. Instead, he just emphatically told Sarah to bring him another two beers. With that, R. V. came over next to Kenny and put a hand on Kenny's shoulder. Kenny knocked it off and went back to his beer, but R. V. put it back. By this point, Kenny had had enough. He stood up, kicked his stool backward, and reached back to prepare to take a roundhouse swing at R. V., but before he could actually throw the punch, Steve Fairchild jumped between them. You know how big and how strong Steve is. With one hand, he was holding back Kenny, and with the other, he had R. V. by the collar. Kenny, from what I was told, was screaming at R. V. that he was going to kill him, and R. V. was doing his best to get through Steve so he could get at Kenny. Steve was doing his best to keep them apart. Sarah, by this time, had discovered what was going on, and she started screaming at both of them to leave.

"R. V. apparently then yelled at her, 'Sarah, you can't throw me out of your damn bar. You know how much I spend in here every week? Well, in case you've forgotten, it's usually about five hundred dollars! You know much Kenny spends in here? Well, how much do two beers a day add up to?'

"Sarah didn't hesitate. She replied: 'R. V., as of this moment, your bar privileges are officially revoked. Now get out of my damn bar before I call the sheriff.' With that, she nodded at Steve, who with one hand deftly grabbed R. V. by the back of his collar, and with the other took hold of the back of his jeans and not so gently lifted him off the ground. Steve carried him past Robert and the other guys R. V. had just bought drinks for. Steve then unceremoniously deposited R. V. outside the back door of the bar. I later heard from Georgia that Robert and the others had made a point of thanking R. V. for the free drink as he was carried past."

"Darn. I wonder what that was really all about. I know Kenny doesn't like R. V. Apparently, the feeling is mutual. What was the other thing you wanted to tell me about?"

"Well," she began, "this one is really something, even by Saint James City standards."

"All right!" I answered. "I'm all ears. Tell me all about it!"

"Strangely enough," she began, "this one involves R. V. as well, and it's kind of hard to believe. But you know that Georgia and R. V.'s wife, Shirley, know each other pretty well, and Georgia says she got this whole story directly from Shirley, so I guess it's true. Anyway, Shirley told Georgia that a package from some company she'd never heard of came in the mail to their house last week. It was addressed using R. V.'s real name, not just his initials, so she assumed it was probably just junk mail and opened it. But it wasn't junk mail. Instead, it was a group of photo proofs sent out by a company that takes pictures from helicopters of boats out on the sound. Apparently, the company's business model is to get the home addresses of the boats' owners from the state's vessel-registration data bank, then send proofs of the pictures they've taken to the owners and offer to provide copies for a fee. Shirley told Georgia that normally she'd just have trashed the offer, but she thought having pictures of his boat might make a nice birthday present for her to give to R. V. That is, until she looked more closely at the pictures."

"Oh, boy! This is going to be good, isn't it?" I asked.

"Oh, yeah. Real good. Upon further inspection, Shirley discovered that, while the pictures were indeed excellent representations of R. V. piloting his boat, they also showed remarkably clear images of a largely undressed Lois Anne Emory displaying her proudest possessions to the camera!"

"What? Her boobs?"

"Yep. Both of them, apparently rather arrogantly presented, one in each hand, for closer inspection by the helicopter's photographer."

"On R. V.'s boat? With R. V.?"

"Yep."

"Was there anyone else on board?" I asked.

"Nope."

"Did Shirley know Lois Anne was going to be on board?"

"Nope."

"Uh-oh!"

"Uh-oh is right," Jill said. "From what Georgia said, Shirley is not happy!"

"Jeez. I reckon she wouldn't be. What's she going to do about it?" I asked.

"Georgia says Shirley says she will never leave R. V. He's got too much money, and they've been together too long, for her to ever do that. And besides, according to Georgia, this isn't the first time R. V. has strayed off the reservation."

"So, if she's not going to leave him, I wonder what she will do."

"Georgia wasn't sure, but she did say that Shirley had ordered a number of copies of the pictures, to be delivered to her confidentially. We all agreed that it sounded like this episode was going to be really, really expensive for someone."

"Wow!" I said. "It sounds to me like R. V. is in a world of trouble."

Chapter Eight

The next several weeks passed quietly. Kenny and I spent much of it helping our friend Rucker prepare for the grouper-fishing expedition he'd promised to take us on as soon as his boat and the weather were both ready. Rucker owns what I consider to be an almost perfect boat for offshore grouper fishing: a vintage, twenty-seven-foot, diesel-powered Shamrock. The boat, while not nearly as fast as more modern vessels, more than makes up for this deficiency by being wide, heavy, stable, and down-right fishable. It features an aft fishing deck, protected by sturdy and high rails, which can easily accommodate four adults, each braced in his or her own corner of the deck, secured against pitching or rolling the sea might inflict on them. The stern of the boat features a well-made pass-through opening, sometimes called a "tuna door," should one ever need to drag aboard a really hefty fish. It also houses a deep live well that does a good job of keeping bait fish alive. Under a deck hatch is a large, self-draining ice locker designed for keeping fresh whatever you catch. Forward of the fishing deck is a large, well-lit cabin that houses the pilot's station, as well as a table and enough cushioned benches to give the whole crew places to sit out of the weather during the long journeys to the grouper-fishing grounds. Farther forward are the head and a set of V-berths, normally used only if someone needs to sleep off a case of mal de mer.

We've both fished Rucker's boat before, so we knew that it would be up to the task of venturing offshore. As we knew, Rucker was meticulous about, and took pride in, keeping his vessel sound and seaworthy. On the other hand, we knew that, despite having owned this boat for years, he was still getting up to speed on how to actually fish for grouper. On some of the previous fishing expeditions we had made with him, Kenny and I both had very carefully dropped hints about things we thought he might do differently and things he might look to acquire in order to be more successful. For example, we'd tried to educate him about how grouper could only be found where there was some sort of structure on the bottom and the importance of positioning the boat on top of such a structure. In this regard, the GPS/sonar system on the boat, while perfectly adequate for the task of getting us to and from where we wanted to go, was a little wanting when compared with the high-tech offerings now on the market. The most glaring shortcomings of his current system were that the sonar did little more than tell you how far the sea floor was beneath the boat. We knew he could, and should, do better. Therefore, we were very glad when we learned that he had finally agreed with our suggestions and had purchased a modern navigation system.

We'd spent several days this week helping him come up to speed on how to operate this complex new electronic marvel. One of the most important initial tasks had been to transfer, via download, Rucker's waypoints (navigation points, as well as grouper numbers) from the old system. This went reasonably well, considering that none of us is either young or technologically savvy. Truthfully, it went a heck of a lot better once Rucker's wife (who *is* technologically savvy) finally took pity on us and came out to do the download for us. After that, we mostly spent a lot of time reading through the operating manual for the new system, arguing about what the instructions meant and how best to implement them. Candidly, none of us really knew that much about what we were discussing, but there must have been some value to our educational method, because by week's end, we all were pretty much up to speed on the jargon and terminology in the manual. And, as any experienced deckhand knows, knowing the lingo is at least half the battle.

Another shortcoming of Rucker's boat, one I'd spent considerable time discussing with him, was that it didn't have an EPIRB. This word is an abbreviation of "Electronic Position Indicating Radio Beacon," an apparatus that, in the opinion of many, is one of the most important lifesaving inventions available today. What the device does, should your boat sink, is release a floating, high-powered radio transponder that will automatically, and continually, broadcast an emergency message, along with your exact position, to the nearest coast guard, or other rescue, resource. With this device, help can be on the way to your location, should you need it, literally within minutes; without it, unless you were somehow miraculously able, in the panicked seconds as your boat is sinking, to contact someone and broadcast your coordinates to them, you are probably not coming home. In my opinion, no boat going out of sight of land, much less fifty miles or more out into the Gulf of Mexico should leave the dock without one. I had tried on several occasions to convince Rucker about the importance of acquiring this device and had finally told him I wasn't going to go fishing with him anymore if he didn't mount one. Now, I was glad to see he finally had. Progress!

Unfortunately, despite our best collective efforts over a period of several days, the newly installed, high-priced, high-tech sonar system on Rucker's boat was failing to impress us. Nothing we had yet tried would enable the new high-resolution display screen to show the floor of the sea in greater detail, or more clearly, than had his old low-tech system. Finally, in defeat, Kenny and I insisted that Rucker call the marina where he'd purchased the system to see if they had any suggestions about what we might try next. While he went to make the call, Kenny and I each cracked a beer.

"Dang," Kenny said, "that's a real pisser. You spend all that money on a new system, and it doesn't show the bottom any better than the one you had. If I was Rucker, I think I'd take the whole thing back."

"You're right about that," I agreed. "But you'd think it would be better. You look at all the pictures in the manual, and it shows you can get all kind of clarity and detail of the bottom. But, hell, all we could get was a solid line. And as far as I could tell, all the settings were correct, and we followed all the instructions properly."

"Yep. Well," Kenny said, laughing, "I sure hope Rucker can get it fixed. We're going to need to be able to see structures on the bottom if we're ever going to be able to catch grouper with him."

"Yep," I agreed. "Now, Kenny, what's this I hear about you getting into it with R. V.?"

"You heard about that, huh?"

"Yep. Jill heard about it at cards and told me. What in the hell happened?"

"Not much. I tried to kill the bastard, but Steve Fairchild stopped me," Kenny said.

"Yeah, I know that. But why did y'all get into it?" I asked.

"The bastard wouldn't buy me a drink."

"Is that all?"

"No," he replied.

He opened his mouth to tell me more but shut it when we heard Rucker coming back onto the dock. Instead, he turned his face toward him and said "Did you get it figured out yet? What were we doing wrong?"

"Apparently, we weren't doing anything wrong. The guy who installed it thinks he forgot to hook up something. I'm going to take the boat to him tomorrow and have him look at it. So, we should be ready to go fishing on Friday. Y'all in?"

"Oh, heck yeah," we answered in near unison.

Chapter Nine

I returned home in time to get a quick kiss from Jill as she left the house, heading for her weekly canasta night with the girls. I noticed that, as is her custom on girls' card night, she had dressed in some of her more fashionable island attire. I smiled at that, knowing the other ladies would be similarly dolled up. It always amused me that when the guys get together in the evenings, while we might have put on clean shorts and fishing shirts, there was nothing really different about the clothes we wore then from what we'd have worn all day. Women, I've noticed, seem to view these types of opportunities for social interaction from another point of view—a perspective that seems to require them to go to some effort to present themselves attractively. I'm sure that anthropologists, having observed the same types of competitive preening in other animal species, would not find this type of behavior surprising. For me, I'm just happy that it seems to make Jill happy. And, besides, I always look forward to seeing her looking good.

"Baby," Jill said, "I went to the Winn-Dixie today and got you some fresh salmon. It's in the fridge, ready to go in the oven. And there's some frozen spinach you can nuke. And, if you want, there's some leftover coleslaw."

"Sounds good, babe. As you very well know, that's just about my favorite meal in the whole world. So, y'all are going to be at Georgia's tonight?"

"Yep. It's her week, and I've been looking forward to it all day. She's a great cook."

"She is that," I agreed. "If there are any leftovers, bring me some."

"Not much chance of that," she said. "And even if there were, I'd have to fight Robert for them."

"Yeah," I said, chuckling in agreement. "Well, at least bring me back some juicy gossip."

I winked, and quickly ducked inside, successfully avoiding what I knew would be an indignant denial. Then, through the door's glass panes, I saw her stick her tongue out and flip me a bird, before turning and happily starting down the outside stairs.

I always look forward to the evenings when I have the house to myself for a few hours. I love my wife very much, and I think she loves me, but in retirement, since you tend to spend so much time together, having a few hours alone is a pleasure. And, besides, card night is the same night that *Moonshiners* comes on TV. I hate to admit this to anyone, but I really love this so-called reality show. I suspect it may have something to do with my Scottish heritage; my southern upbringing; and, without question, my love for scotch whisky. I had just finished cleaning up the dishes and was pouring myself a third "wee dram" of some of Scotland's finest when I heard Jill pull in the driveway.

As she opened the door to the kitchen, I welcomed her home and advised her to hurry up since the evening's featured new *Moonshiners* airing was about to start. I had expected Jill, as is her norm, to head upstairs to change into something more comfortable. I was a little surprised when she came in, sat on the couch, and turned toward me, her face beaming like the Cheshire cat's. I knew that meant she had indeed brought home some particularly tasty gossip, news that she couldn't wait to share.

"Uh-oh," I said. "What's up?"

"You are not going to believe what I heard tonight!"

"Probably," I agreed. "But can this wait? The new *Moonshiners* is about to start."

I had said this just to be a little bit aggravating; truthfully, I was as interested in hearing the news as she was excited to share it with me. But I knew that a little bit of stage management would help to make the eventual disclosure even better.

"Fine! You just watch your damn show, and I'll go upstairs to change," Jill responded.

"Wait," I quickly replied. "I was just kidding! What'd you hear?"

"No," she countered. "I know you don't want to miss the latest adventures of Bill and Jim Tom."

"No, baby. I'll turn this off. I do want to hear what you've got to say."

I surreptitiously pressed the record button before making a more dramatic production of turning off the TV.

"See, I told you I want to hear your news. What's going on?"

"Well, OK…you remember what I told you a couple of weeks ago that Georgia had told me about how R. V. Dodge's wife had gotten pictures from a helicopter company? The ones that showed R. V. and Lois Anne Emory together on R. V.'s boat?"

"Yeah," I answered, already suspecting that what I was about to hear next was going to be especially attention-grabbing. "What'd she do about that?"

"Georgia says Shirley ordered several sets of the prints. She gave one to her attorney; one to R. V., who I understand is now staying at their house in Labelle; and she gave another set to Mack Emory, Lois Anne's husband. According to Georgia, he was not at all happy to learn about their indiscretion. She said the first thing he did was call his attorney. Then he went home, had it out with Lois Anne, packed his stuff, and moved out. Georgia thinks he went back to Labelle, too. But, and this is the best part, apparently, he'd just sold a really large shipment of liquid-nitrogen fertilizer to R. V.'s farm. But, for some strange reason, when R. V.'s guys sprayed it on his watermelons, they all died."

"What? They died? How many died? And what killed them?"

"Georgia said that she'd heard from Robert that R. V. lost a couple thousand acres of melons. From what Robert said, although there was no way to prove it after the fact, R. V. suspects that Mack had spiked the shipment of fertilizer that was delivered to R. V.'s farm with Roundup. According to Georgia, R. V. is livid. Apparently, the melons that died were going to be the first to hit market this year, and they would have fetched top dollar. She said this disaster will easily cost R. V. a couple of million dollars."

"Damn! That's a lot of money. So what's R. V. going to do about it?"

"Georgia says he is suing Mack and Mack's company as well. In addition, the word around Hendry County is that he's promised to whip Mack's ass the next time they meet."

"I don't know about that," I replied. "I think I'd put my money on Mack Emory."

"Yeah, I would, too," Jill responded. "In that regard, Georgia also said she'd heard that the word on the street in Labelle is that Mack has promised to knock R. V.'s brains out the next time they meet."

"He actually threatened to knock R. V.'s brains out?"

"Yeah. And, according to Georgia, that's not all. She said Robert told her Mack had promised to use his knife to turn R. V. into a gelding, whatever that means."

"Oh, jeez," I replied. "You really don't know what that means?"

"I think it means he's going to castrate him," she said.

"Yeah. My guess would be that he actually plans to cut it all off," I answered.

Chapter Ten

Thursday afternoon late, I picked up Kenny in my boat. We'd made plans to cast net an ample supply of pinfish for the following day's grouper fishing on Rucker's boat. Usually, getting a supply of this kind of bait is fairly easy to do. All that's required is to find an expanse of healthy sea grass growing in about four or five feet of clear water. Then, once the anchor is down, you start to throw out small balls of moistened chum into the area just up-current of where you intend to throw your net.

Cast netting is something most crackers learn to do at a young age. I remember well the first lessons I got from my father about how to throw a net. We'd gone out in the backyard of our house. He'd had his ten-foot mullet net, while I'd had the little six-foot mullet net he'd gotten me for Christmas. I can't be sure now how old I actually was then—maybe eight or nine—but I remember thinking at that time that that ten-foot net was enormous. But my dad was a big man, and he could throw that thing without any problem. Heck, I remember he could even throw it when he was wading in water above his knees, stalking mullet as they warily schooled nearby. Heck, my dad even had a twelve-foot mullet net, but even he could successfully open that one only from a bridge or a pier.

The secret to getting a cast net to reliably open is that you have to get the lead line around the bottom of the net to spin so that centrifugal force opens the net for you. There are a lot of different ways cast netters make that happen. The method I learned from my father was to grip the net so the bottom three feet or so were hanging down. Then, pick up the lead line near your right leg with your right hand and put that in your mouth, gripping it lightly between your front teeth. Some people, for whatever reason, don't like to do this, so an alternative approach is to lay this section of lead line over your right shoulder. The downside of this latter approach is that you will soon be soaking wet. Regardless, the next step is to reach down with your right hand, grip the lead line that's hanging down, and flip several sections of the net back over your right arm or leg. You want to end up with at least a third of the net separated from the rest of the net in this fashion. You then grasp this section of net in your right hand, holding the lead line itself between your thumb and first finger. Now you are ready to cast the net. To actually make the throw, you place your right foot ahead of your body and your left foot behind it, and then slowly twist your body around to the left, keeping your left elbow in close to your side, and allowing your right hand to follow the net. Then, when you are ready, you twist rapidly to the right, allowing the bottom of the net to spin away from your body. As the net begins to rotate, you straighten your arms to throw or push the net in the direction you want it to go. Finally, you use your right hand's grip on the lead line to impart a little extra spin on the net. And what about the section of net clenched loosely between your teeth? Truthfully, for me, it always just comes out without my even being conscious of it, but I know some folks are so fixated on this that they have a hard time doing anything else. My advice is to just let your teeth take care of themselves. And that's all there is to throwing a net.

Down here, there are basically two kinds of cast nets: mullet nets and bait nets. The only difference is the size of the mesh that makes up the net. A larger mesh allows smaller fish to escape the net. For mullet, you use a one-and-a-quarter-inch mesh; for bait, a quarter-inch mesh is required. Anything larger than that allows white bait to gill themselves in the net, creating a nightmare as they get their heads through the net's openings, but since their bodies are too large to follow, the net's mesh embeds itself in the fishes' gills when they try to back out. The result is a net festooned with hundreds of trapped fish, doomed to death as the only option for the fisherman is to literally squeeze the heads off the fish in order to remove them from the net.

Today we weren't worried about white bait, which normally we'd only catch in shallower water, typically near sandbars. We were after pinfish, one of the universal baits in Southwest Florida. We'd been chumming for ten minutes when I decided to make my first, and as it turned out only, cast. Almost as soon as the net settled to the bottom, I could see that the throw had been successful. Silver flashes sparkled from the opaque water as dozens of fish searched frantically for an escape. And then, as soon as I began to tighten the handline that pulls up the leads that connect around the bottom of the net, I could feel the impacts from dozens of panicked fish as they realized there was no way out of the shrouds of billowing mesh that enveloped them. When I lifted the net clear of the water, I could see what I estimated to easily be over fifty pinfish—more than enough for our needs tomorrow.

Kenny and I sorted through the haul and quickly stowed the flopping bait in the boat's live well. Then I shook out the net and folded it back into the five-gallon bucket in which it normally resided. I'd wash it when I got home. While I was doing that, Kenny was thoroughly washing down the boat to rid it of the seaweed that inevitably comes aboard anytime you throw a net. We weren't in a hurry, as we knew the fish would survive the short trip to Rucker's house. With our chores completed, I eased the boat onto a plane, and Kenny used his cell to alert Rucker that we were on the way.

Minutes later, we idled up the short canal that leads from the bay toward Rucker's house. He was standing on the dock waiting for us. As we eased alongside the dock, he grabbed the bow line that Kenny tossed him and made it secure on a cleat. He then did the same with the stern line I handed to him.

"So y'all were able to get some bait, huh?" Rucker asked.

Kenny responded with gleeful delight, "One cast! That's all it took. Just one cast, and Captain Story had all the pinfish we could want. I'm telling you, that man knows what he's doing."

"Well, let's hope he knows how to catch grouper tomorrow, too," Rucker responded.

"Rucker, that ain't my responsibility!" I replied. "Let me remind you that it's *your* job to find the fish."

"Well, that's not going to be a problem, now that I've got my new equipment," he laughingly answered. "With this new technology, all we'll have to do is just drive around and wait until we see a big one swim by. It should be a piece of cake."

"Well, I hope so. Now, hand me your bucket and let's get these pinfish into your bait pen."

Five minutes later, that task was accomplished, and we were all three sipping the cold beers that Rucker had thoughtfully provided. Actually, he had overlooked producing said beverages until Kenny had irritably, but gently, reminded him of his traditional responsibilities as a host in Saint James City. Fortunately, Rucker rose to the occasion and even made up for this oversight by quickly producing refills when the first bottles had been drained. We spent a companionable thirty minutes enjoying the beers and discussing plans for the upcoming trip off shore. I was especially pleased to hear that Rucker planned to fish some new numbers he'd recently acquired from a guy down at Froggy's—numbers the guy had promised would produce a lot of fish. I was looking forward to the trip.

Chapter Eleven

The morning dawned bright and clear. A cold front that had worked its way across the peninsula earlier in the week had moved on to the Bahamas, leaving behind a dome of high pressure and glorious weather. In the immediate aftermath of the front's passing, we had experienced a few days of a boisterous northerly wind as the pressure gradients equalized. But today's forecast called for a light easterly breeze. I thought that all of this promised a perfect day for venturing into the gulf.

We had agreed to rendezvous at Rucker's dock at 7:00 a.m. As I drove up to the house, I saw Kenny's SUV parked in front of the house, on the verge of the cul-de-sac. I was not surprised. I knew he was habitually an early riser. I also knew he was always impatient to get fishing trips under way. To him, a minute spent at the dock was a minute wasted. As I walked through the yard and around the corner of the house, I noticed Kenny carrying a couple of five-gallon buckets of ice from Rucker's ice-making machine to the boat. As I walked up, he handed them to Rucker, who was standing in the fishing cockpit.

"Good morning, gentlemen," I said. "Looks like you guys have already been hard at work."

Rucker emptied the buckets into the fish locker, which I noticed was now full of ice, before replying, "This ain't work! We're getting ready to go fishing—this is fun."

"You've got that right," I replied. "Now what can I do to help?"

"Oh, nothing," Rucker said. "You just get your sleepy ass on board. We're ready to shove off right now. We've got some grouper to catch."

I noticed that Kenny was already holding the untied dock line in his hand, impatiently waiting for Rucker's signal to bring it aboard.

As I stepped down into the cockpit, I asked, "Y'all got the pinfish loaded? How are they doing?"

"Yep," Rucker responded. "They all look healthy. We didn't lose a single fish overnight."

"Beer, water, and food on board?" I asked.

"Come on, Jim," Kenny interrupted. "Will you get aboard and stow your gear so we can get going? We're burning daylight."

"OK. OK. Hold your horses," I answered, as I put my rod in the appropriate rack and slid my tackle bag into an out-of-the-way corner of the cabin.

Seconds later, Kenny was on board, and the boat's diesel-engine exhaust was comfortably burbling in the water as Rucker idled the Shamrock backward out of the slip. Then, once clear of the dock, he eased the transmission into forward, and we were under way. Initially, our progress was slow as we wakelessly made our way out of the canal. Then, as we entered the slow speed zone, Rucker fed in a little more throttle, to which the diesel responded with what could have been a happy murmur. Finally, four or five long minutes later, we reached the resume safe speed zone. Rucker looked at us all to check that we were braced for acceleration. Seeing that we were, he took a long look up and down the channel to ensure there was not any approaching traffic. Seeing none, he uttered "OK, y'all hold on, here we go."

He smoothly pushed the throttle farther forward with a progressive motion. The engine responded to this input with an eager growl. The boat's stern settled deeper into the water as the power from the engine forced it down. Then, as the hull gathered speed, the boat began its climb onto the top of the water's surface. Seconds later, we were on a smooth plane, the boat seemingly pleased and proud to once again be heading to sea. Rucker calmly adjusted the engine's RPMs to achieve the targeted speed.

To me there is something comforting and reassuring about the deep-throated thrumming a marine diesel engine makes as it pushes a boat through the water. Without doubt, this low-pitched resonance conveys both power and strength. But the unwavering, constant revolutions of a diesel somehow also suggest a greater degree of steadiness and purposefulness than that conveyed by the frenetic, complicated, and highly stressed noises emitted by gasoline engines. Without question, power, strength, comfort, and reassurance are all good things to feel when you are on a boat heading to sea. It's a sound that I very much enjoy hearing.

As we cleared Redfish Pass, I stood next to the captain's chair so I could get a look at where Rucker was piloting us. As I gazed at the impressive display panel of his newfangled chart plotter, I was amazed at the clarity and detail produced by the device. I was impressed. Looking more closely, I could see that the boat was on a course due west, with a distance to travel of just under fifty miles. I smiled to myself, recognizing that where we were heading was remarkably near the spot to which I had traveled on Mack Emory's boat not long ago. Apparently, Mack's concern that the number might become widely spread by R. V. Dodge did indeed have merit. I just hoped there were still some fish left on it.

Armed with my new knowledge about where we were going, I began to look around at the gulf. The last time I had been on this course, I remembered, I had been stunned by an ethereal display of changing colors as the morning's ocean haze transitioned from dusk to daylight. Today I didn't see that. Instead, all I saw was bright, sparkling sunshine reflecting off the surface of a smooth, almost mirrorlike sea. Beautiful still, but entirely different. I guessed that today's low atmospheric humidity, a product of the surrounding high-pressure zone, together with our being at this spot at a slightly later time of day, was responsible for the variation.

Kenny, I noticed, was already curled up asleep in one corner of the cabin. I considered doing the same but concluded that leaving Rucker alone to monitor the boat's progress as the new autopilot steered us unwaveringly out to the fishing spot would be rude. Instead, I decided to engage him in conversation.

"Beautiful day, huh, Rucker?" I asked.

"Fantastic!" he replied. "You couldn't ask for a nicer one. It's about time the wind died down. I was afraid we were going to have to postpone the trip."

"Yeah. Me, too," I replied. "I don't like to do the gulf when it's bumpy. By the way, I can't help but be impressed with how your new autopilot is behaving. There's none of that weaving around that you had with your old unit. This one's steering straight as an arrow."

"I know. This is great. Now, I hope the new sonar is going to work as well. I'm really looking forward to being able to see the structure on the bottom."

"Speaking of structure on the bottom, I'm impressed with the spot to which it looks like we're heading. If I'm not mistaken, it seems a lot like the spot I fished with Mack Emory a month or so ago. We caught our limit of nice grouper that day. You said you bought it off a guy at Froggy's?"

"Bartered would be more like it." Rucker chuckled. "You know, timing really is everything. I was down at the bar sitting next to this guy. I didn't know him, but we got to talking, mostly about fishing stuff. Well, apparently, this guy had been at the bar for a while before I arrived. He was beginning to slur his words slightly and was also starting to have a little trouble staying on his stool. I told the lady tending bar that I'd like to buy him a drink, but when she delivered it, she told him she thought he'd had enough, and that the Old Grand-Dad and water she'd just served would have to be his last. To his credit, he took the news without making a fuss."

"This is the guy you got the numbers from?" I asked.

"Yeah," Rucker answered. "I mentioned that I liked Old Grand-Dad, too. And then added, that in fact, I happened to have in the car a bottle I'd just bought that morning down at Doc Watson's. When I said that, his eyes lit up, and he asked me if I needed a good grouper number. Of course, I said yes but began to question him closely about whether a number I got from him would be any good. I was really just trying to blow him off at that point. I didn't want to squander a perfectly good bottle of old-school bourbon on fake grouper coordinates. But then he started to tell me about how he'd gotten the spot, and I began to believe that maybe there was something to his story. Long story short, we went out to the car. He pulled out his cell phone and gave me the location. I gave him the fifth of liquor. I guess we'll find out in a little while whether I made a good trade or not."

"Well, from what I can tell by looking at the chart, I think you probably made a very good trade," I replied. "Did you know this guy?"

"No. I just happened to sit down beside him at the bar. He told me he'd gotten the numbers from some loudmouth asshole who was bragging down at the bar about how many grouper he'd pulled off this spot. He said this guy claimed that he and some of his buddies had fished this spot a couple of times recently, and each time they had limited out."

"So," I asked, "this loudmouth just gave him the numbers?"

"Not exactly," Rucker replied. "According to my friend at the bar, first he had to buy the guy five Dewar's and waters. But, eventually, the loudmouth came to the conclusion that he and my friend were bosom buddies. To thank him for the drinks, he gave my guy the number. But who knows if it's really any good or not?"

"From a reliable source like that, it has to be good!" I laughed.

"Yeah. It's got to be good," Rucker agreed.

After that, we just shot the breeze. Mainly we talked about Rucker's boat and his new navigation system. Finally, as we approached the designated location to which we had been heading, Rucker throttled back the engine and began to slowly idle toward the targeted spot. When the engine note changed, Kenny woke up.

"We in Mexico yet?" he asked.

"Almost," Rucker replied. "Come over here, look at this depth finder, and tell me what you see."

"Damn!" Kenny and I both exclaimed.

Kenny added, "That looks like structure extraordinaire to me."

"I agree," said Rucker. "I'd say we drop the anchor and go fishing."

"Let's do it," Kenny eagerly replied.

Then, even before the anchor had settled on the bottom, Kenny stuck a flopping, protesting pinfish onto his forged grouper hook and sent it on its way to what he hoped would be a rendezvous with a large, healthy black or red grouper.

And that's exactly what happened. Before he'd even had time to properly position the weight above the bottom, Kenny was pulling back against what had to have been a sizable grouper. As we watched, he was trying his best to keep the fish from reaching the security of the rocks on the bottom. It took Kenny the better part of five minutes to win the fight and bring the fish to the surface. By that time, Kenny was breathing hard. Rucker and I both, on different occasions, had offered to relieve Kenny, suggesting as we did that we were concerned he might not be enough of a man to subdue the fish. Kenny, of course, would have none of it. His colorful, and profane, replies to our offers made it quite clear that he didn't need our help.

As the fish neared the surface, Rucker and Kenny began to debate whether we needed to use a gaff to bring the fish aboard. I quickly decided this issue by reaching down with a landing net to lift the struggling fish into the boat. As the fish flounced unhappily against the bottom of the boat, we knew there was no reason to measure it. This fish had to have been thirty inches, if it was an inch. I quickly pulled open the lid to the ice locker, and Kenny calmly used the side of his foot to guide the unfortunate grouper into the waiting hole.

"Dang, Kenny," I exclaimed. "That was a heck of a fish. I'm glad you took a nap on the way out here. Otherwise, I'm afraid that fish would have been too much for you to handle."

"Stuff yourself, Jim," Kenny replied. "Now, get out my way, so I can get to the live well. I need another pinfish."

"You just wait your turn," I told him. "I've got to get one first."

Then Rucker added, "And let me in there, too. Why don't you take a break? You look like you could use one."

"Y'all just hurry up and get your bait, then get out of my way. I've got fish to catch!" Kenny responded.

Over the next hour we brought on board numerous legal keepers. We threw back probably twice that number of fish, which were below the minimum length requirement. Truthfully, by this time, we all needed to take a break. We needed to stretch our backs and shake out the cramps that had begun to develop in our forearms and biceps. We each put our rods aside and were soon enjoying either bottled waters or cold beers. Rucker had taken his place in the helmsman's chair, and I was standing beside him. We were inspecting the view of the bottom provided by his new depth sounder. I was impressed. I had just made a suggestion about how he might be able to tweak the resolution of the picture when we heard Kenny's voice from on deck.

"What the heck is that? Y'all come out here and take a look at this."

Rucker and I stepped outside and took a place on either side of Kenny, trying to see what he had just seen.

"What is it, Kenny?" I asked.

"I don't know," he replied. "At first I thought it was a jellyfish, but then I wasn't so sure. It was down about seven or eight feet, but I don't see it now."

"Could it have been a big fish?" Rucker inquired.

"Maybe, but it didn't really look like that. Wait…there it is! Do y'all see it now?"

"I do see something," I said. "But I'm not sure what it is. For a minute, I thought it was a crab trap, but it was too colorful for that, and it's not shaped exactly like a crab trap—"

"I see it, too!" Rucker interrupted. "We've got to find out what that is. Kenny, why don't you grab the long-handled gaff, and let's see if we can reach it."

"OK! Let me get it out of the rack," Kenny agreed.

As he lowered the sharp-hooked gaff into the water, I said, "Kenny, I want to see what this is, too, but all I've got to say is that you'd better not bring up another damn corpse like you did last year. That, if you remember, almost got us killed."

"And it smelled pretty bad, too," Kenny mumbled, almost to himself.

"It is not a corpse," Rucker interjected. "Come on—gaff it, Kenny, and let's find out what it is. Maybe it's an old weather balloon. Or, who knows, it could be a square grouper."

"There's no way we'd ever be that lucky!" I said, half-jokingly.

By this time, Kenny had extended the telescoping gaff pole to its full length, and had begun sweeping it in the general vicinity of where we had last seen the submerged object.

For a couple of minutes, he found nothing, and just when we were about ready to write off all hopes of ever seeing what we had glimpsed, Kenny said, "Uh-oh!"

Rucker said, "What do you mean, 'uh-oh'? Have you got something?"

"Yeah," Kenny said hesitantly. "But I don't really like the feel of what I've got."

"What does it feel like?" I asked.

"It's big, and it's heavy, and it's kind of squishy," he replied. "It kind of reminds me of that time when we were tarpon fishing."

"Uh-oh!" I said.

"Will y'all stop that?" Rucker urged. "Can you pull it up, Kenny?"

"I think so, but…I'm not really sure I want to," Kenny replied.

"Damn it, Kenny! Quit messing around with that thing before we lose it," Rucker insisted. "Let me help you pull that pole up, and let's get that thing to the top."

Together, Kenny and Rucker fed the pole upward through their hands, gradually working the weight toward the surface. As the object came nearer, we began to make out its colors. I could see what looked like a light hue on a portion of the thing, and then what looked like yellow, and blue—almost like the bright colors of a fish called a tang, but much larger than any tang I'd ever seen. And there was something else, but I couldn't make it out.

"Come on, Kenny," Rucker encouraged. "Don't stop now. We've almost got it to the surface. What do y'all think it is?"

"I don't have a clue," I said.

Kenny didn't say anything, but he continued to feed the pole upward through his hands. Finally, the mystery object broke the surface, and then, unfortunately, there was no doubt.

"Oh, heck!" I heard Kenny exclaim.

I heard Rucker retching overboard.

"Damn. Not again!" was all I said.

Chapter Twelve

There's something about pulling the dead body of one of your fellow humans out of the water that will ruin any day of fishing. This was the second time Kenny and I had performed this task. We hadn't enjoyed it the first time, and we certainly weren't happy about it now, either.

A couple of years ago, Kenny and I had been fishing for tarpon in the deep channel that leads under the third span of the Sanibel Causeway when we hooked a mutilated corpse that had, shortly before, been a happy young man who had come to the island to attend the wedding of one of his buddies. That episode, as it played out, had almost gotten Kenny and me killed. I had no desire to relive that experience. I doubt Kenny wanted to, either.

When we dragged up that first body, it was a simple matter to call the Lee County Sheriff's Department and hand the matter (and the body) off to them as quickly as possible. This time, though, we were fifty miles out in the Gulf of Mexico, clearly not in Lee County. Hell, technically we weren't even in the United

States. The first thought running through my head as the guy dangled on the sharp end of Kenny's gaff was, *Who in the hell do we call now?*

Then I thought, *Should we call anyone? Would it be better just to let the poor guy drop back down into the gulf?* Before I could seriously consider that action, Kenny answered the question for us.

When he and Rucker had pulled the guy up from the gulf, the body had been facedown. At first glance, we could tell it was obviously a Caucasian man's body—probably, we guessed, the body of a well-fed, middle-aged guy. We could see he was naked from the waist down. The upper portion of his body was covered by what looked to be a yellow- and blue-striped golf shirt. That was about all we could see, because his head was hanging down into the water. At that point, what we had brought to the surface was the half-naked body of a man we didn't know.

At that point, it would have been not too difficult a decision to simply let the body slip off the gaff and let it go back to swimming with the fish. But that was before Kenny turned the corpse over. Once he turned the body over, we no longer had the option of choosing not to become involved: we actually knew the guy.

"What in the hell happened to him?" asked Rucker, now recovered enough to look again at what was on the gaff.

"Jeez," was all I could say, almost speechless at what we were seeing.

"You boys know who that is, don't you?" asked Kenny, beads of perspiration now on his forehead even though he didn't seem to be hot.

"I think so," I answered, "but I can't be sure. I don't think I've ever seen him with his mouth closed."

Kenny laughed nervously in agreement.

"It looks to me like somebody has sewn his mouth shut," Rucker replied.

"Yep," Kenny said. "They sewed it shut, nice and neat. Y'all see what was used to sew it?"

"Looks like a grouper rig to me," I answered.

"Me, too," replied Kenny. "Strong forged circle hook, fluoro-carbon leader, swivels, orange beads, and a heavy piece of lead... that's a grouper rig, if I've ever seen one."

"Do his cheeks look kind of funny to you?" asked Rucker.

"A little bit," I said. "Kind of full, but who knows? Maybe that's just from him starting to swell up, or something."

"Or something," said Kenny. "What else y'all see?"

"Well, I guess it's more like what I don't see," I said.

"Exactly!" Kenny replied. "Rucker, do you see what we're talking about?"

But Rucker couldn't answer, because he was leaning over the gunwale and throwing up again.

"Damn, Kenny!" I replied. "It looks like somebody cut the poor guy's dick off."

"Either that, or a shark was a mite picky about what morsel he went for first. But, to me, it looks like it was cut off with a sharp knife."

"So we're thinking," I asked, "that somebody cut the guy's member off, stuffed it in his mouth, sewed his lips together using a grouper rig, and dumped his body to feed the fish on this world-class grouper hole?"

"That sounds about right to me," answered Kenny. "What does that suggest to you?"

"One theory suggested by these facts," I said, "would be that this guy probably screwed someone's wife, stole his grouper numbers, and then talked too much, and too loudly, about having done those things."

"That line of reasoning, given what we know about this guy, would seem to make perfect sense," agreed Kenny.

"So, y'all *do* know who this guy is?" asked Rucker.

"Yeah," I replied. "And you do, too, don't you?"

"I think so. It looks to me like that loudmouth who was at Georgia and Robert's party a couple of weeks ago. What was his name?"

Kenny and I answered in unison, "R. V. Dodge!"

Chapter Thirteen

"OK! What do we do now?" Rucker asked.

"If we were back home," I said, "we'd just call Mike Collins in the sheriff's department and let him deal with everything. Lord knows, we've had to do that before. But, jeez, out here I don't know. I mean we're not even in the United States! I wouldn't think this would be in his jurisdiction. What do you guys think we should do?"

"Maybe we should call the coast guard?" Rucker volunteered.

"Maybe," I agreed. "I wouldn't think this is really their jurisdiction, either. And from what I've been reading in the paper recently, if it doesn't have to do with saving someone in imminent danger of losing their life or fighting terrorism, they don't want to get involved anymore."

Hearing that, Kenny spoke up. "Looks to me like old R. V. is beyond being able to benefit from their services in that regard."

Rucker and I chuckled nervously, and I answered, "I don't think there's any question about that. So you don't think we ought to try to contact the coast guard?"

Kenny responded, "Well, I don't know about that. Maybe we should, maybe we shouldn't. To tell you the truth, sometimes those guys kind of give me the willies. Besides, if we call them you know how long we'll have to be out here waiting on them? And then, when they get here, they'll probably put us in hand-cuffs and guard us with their damn machine guns while they try to figure out what's really going down. There's no telling where things might go from there. Hell, they might even take our fish. If it were up to me, I wouldn't call those dudes."

"Well," I said, "what do you think we should do?"

"We could always just leave him here," Kenny replied.

Rucker and I stared at him. Rucker's mouth was now hang-ing open, shocked at the suggestion Kenny had just made—a course of action that I had indeed thought about but, before Kenny said it out loud, not one that I'd seriously considered implementing.

"Kenny," I began, "I don't think—"

"Wait a minute," Kenny interrupted. "Let's just think about this logically for a minute before we leap to any conclusions. Jim, what happened the last times we managed to get ourselves involved in the middle of murder investigations?"

"Well, we did almost get killed," I answered.

"Exactly," Kenny responded. "And, quite honestly, a couple of times the only reason that *didn't* happen is because one or both of us just got lucky. How's your luck been running lately?"

"Well, none of the scratch-offs I've bought at the general store have paid off for a while," I replied.

"Come on, guys! You can't be serious about leaving R. V. out here," said Rucker. "That just wouldn't be right."

I glanced at Kenny and gave him a covert wink. Then I answered Rucker, "Well, none of us really knew R. V. all that well…"

Kenny picked up the deception deftly, replying, "Yeah, and truthfully, he did have a loud mouth, so whoever did this kind of did us all a favor."

"And, besides, from what I've heard about how R. V. has been entertaining himself lately, his wife might not actually miss him all that much."

Rucker was looking at us like we'd lost our minds. He'd opened his mouth to argue when I interrupted to let him off the hook.

"Rucker, we're just kidding with you. We know that, even as much as we might like to, we can't just leave R. V.'s body out here. You're the captain, though, so it's technically your call how we should handle this. My suggestion would be that we load R. V. on the boat and head back to Lee County. When we get within cell-phone range, we can call Mike Collins and have him meet us somewhere where we can hand the body off to them. R. V. was a Lee County resident, and personally, I'd feel better if I knew that Collins was on the case rather than some nautical MP with no knowledge of, or ties to, Pine Island. What do you think?"

"Hey, we've got to do something," Rucker responded, looking relieved that someone had finally made a suggestion he could support. "Let's get him on board."

"OK," I said. "Now, how are we going to do that?"

Kenny weighed in. "I think we ought to put a line around his shoulders and just pull him in through that tuna door on the stern. I'd think we should be able to get him aboard without damaging him too much."

"That sounds like a good plan to me," Rucker said. "Jim, grab one of those dock lines. Kenny, use the gaff to pull R. V. up alongside the swim platform."

I grabbed a line and used a bowline knot to fashion a large loop to slide over R. V. As Kenny held the body secure, I knelt down on the swim deck and slipped the circle around the upper portion of the corpse, getting a bad case of the heebie-jeebies as I had to lift one of R. V.'s floating, unresponsive arms to maneuver the line around him. I was glad I had to touch him only once before the loop was secure. I handed the bitter end of the line to Rucker and asked him to hold pressure on the line as I opened the door. As soon as the line was secure, Kenny positioned himself where he could best assist Rucker in dragging the body aboard. I stayed on the platform to help lift R. V.'s head and shoulders onto the deck.

"All right, guys," I instructed. "I'll tell y'all when to start pulling as soon as I have him positioned on the platform. From there, we'll just have to play it by ear."

I heard Rucker and Kenny mumble their acquiescence to this plan. I positioned my feet where I would best be able to grab the loop and lift it upward as they pulled. By this time, R. V.'s body was again floating facedown, having flipped over as Kenny and I secured the line behind his shoulders. I spread my feet as widely as I could without unduly compromising my ability to lift. My plan was to straddle R. V.'s body as it came aboard, letting Rucker and Kenny pull him between my legs until enough of the body was on deck that I could move around and help them pull.

"OK, guys. On the count of three, y'all start pulling," I said. "One…two…two and a half…"

At that, everyone started laughing.

"Damn it, Jim! Quit that. This is serious business," Rucker said. "We've to get this over with."

"All right," I said. "Just wanted to give you one more chance to reconsider."

"Just lift, damn it. We'll pull."

"OK," I said. "On three. One…two…" I lifted. "Three!"

Rucker and Kenny pulled, and the plan worked. The back of R. V.'s dripping head, and then his wet upper body, slipped between my legs. Before they could reposition for another tug on the line, I yelled at them to stop. "Wait a minute! Y'all stop pulling for a minute, and come look at this."

"Damn it, Jim!" Rucker said. "It's not funny this time. We need to get him on board. Now, quit messing around, and come help us pull him on deck."

"Rucker, I'm not goofing around. Y'all need to see this. When R. V.'s head went past me, I saw something we need to take a look at. Kenny, hold that line tight, and Rucker, you come over here, take a look at the back of his head, and tell me what you see."

"All right, all right, if that'll make you happy. Kenny, you keep a tight grip on that rope. Don't let him slip back into the gulf."

Rucker stepped over to where R. V.'s head was lying facedown on the deck and knelt down to take a look.

"Rucker," I inquired. "What does that look like to you?"

"Dang!" he replied. "It looks to me like there are a couple of pretty deep impressions in his skull, maybe a half inch deep, an inch wide, and a couple of inches long. You thinking that's what did him in?"

"That would be my guess," I replied. "In fact, I'd bet that some-one bashed in the back of his head with a shark bat while they were out here fishing, then did the rest of the stuff to him. At least, I *hope* that's the order that things went down. I'd hate to think that someone gave him that circumcision and sewed his lips shut while R. V. was still alive."

As Rucker and I silently contemplated the horror of that possible scenario, Kenny bought us back to the present, interjecting, "I could use a little help here. How about if we leave the hypothesizing to the investigators and instead concentrate on the job at hand—namely, sliding our friend here onto the deck? And, lest anyone forget, the sooner we can make that happen, the less chance R. V. will begin to...*ripen* on us. It's going to be bad enough having to look at him all the way back to shore. I don't want to have to smell him, too!"

Rucker and I moved to help Kenny drag R. V. on board. And then, as soon as the body was secure and the tuna door closed, Rucker pulled a rain slicker from a locker in the cabin and laid it over the body. Kenny and I secured the edges of the coat from blowing in the wind by rolling one side of R. V. up and letting the body back down on top of the jacket. When we finished with one side, we did the other. We agreed that, while touching him wasn't much fun, it was better than having to watch him flop around on deck every time the boat bounced as we motored back to shore. As soon as that task was complete, we joined Rucker in the cabin. When we stepped inside, he handed us each a cold beer.

"Y'all look like you could use this," he said.

We both nodded and muttered our heartfelt thanks.

"Now, let's get the hell out of here," I said. "Let me know as soon as we have cell service."

Chapter Fourteen

A little over two hours later, just as the boat was about to enter Redfish Pass, I was gently shaken awake by Rucker. Truthfully, I didn't mind being woken up, as my nap had not been altogether pleasant. Rather than having rested, I'd remembered that, as I dreamed, I had been arguing at one time with a creature that had resembled a beautiful, yet frightening, angel of death, and at another, with a thing that, had it not been so hilariously, outrageously funny, I would have sworn was the very devil himself. Now that I was awake, I couldn't remember all we had been discussing, but I could remember that generally we had been disagreeing about the value of my mortal soul. I thought I could recall that they both had taken the position that it was worth far, far less than the value I placed on it. In fact, I seemed to remember that, at one point in the discussion, Lucifer had actually suggested *I* would have to pay *him* in order for him to even consider granting me entrance into the kingdom of hell. As I said, I remembered that the guy was a load of laughs!

"Hey, Jim! Are you awake? We've got cell service now." I shook my head, eventually realizing it was Rucker, rather than Beelzebub, asking the question.

"Yeah, I'm awake. Thanks, Rucker."

"Man, you had me worried there for a while," he said.

"How come?" I asked.

"Well, you were talking in your sleep to beat the band."

"Oh, shit. What'd I say? Did I say anything I shouldn't have said?"

"Well, it's probably a good thing Jill wasn't here. For a while, you were talking up some hot chick, but apparently that didn't go so well, since eventually you started to tell her to go screw herself. That went on for quite some time. Then you just started laughing out loud. I don't know what was so funny, but you sure seemed to be enjoying yourself."

"I don't remember a damn thing," I lied. "I'm going to see if I can get in touch with Mike Collins."

I slid open my phone and scrolled down until I found his number. He answered on the third ring.

"Collins," he responded gruffly.

I remembered from our previous conversations that this was his typical greeting style. For an instant, I seriously considered just hanging up and asking Rucker to head back out to sea so we could secretly and silently commit R. V.'s remains to the deep. But then I realized that the lead investigator of the Lee County Sheriff's Department's Gulf Islands Division would have, by then, had my cell number embedded in the memory of his received-calls list. I also knew that he, being the diligent and curious investigator that he is, eventually would return my call. And that I, being the obvious transparent liar that I am, would immediately incriminate myself. So with that quick assessment out of the way, I replied, "Mike, this is Jim Story."

"Oh, crap!" was his heartfelt response.

Never having had the pleasure of having one of my introductions responded to in this exact manner, I assumed he probably thought he had fumbled the connection and was just expressing his displeasure at having done so. I decided to try again.

"Mike, this is Jim Story."

"I heard you the first time, Story. Actually, I was hoping you had misdialed, and I wouldn't really have to talk with you. But my luck has never been that good. Now, to what do I owe this pleasure?"

"Mike, first let me ask you what is a *purely* hypothetical question."

"Purely hypothetical, huh?"

"Absolutely. If a person, hypothetically speaking, of course, were to find a dead body in the gulf, at a distance that's, let's say, well beyond the twelve-mile limit, what law enforcement organization would have jurisdiction over the investigation?"

For a long, long moment, I heard nothing. Finally, I thought I could hear Collins let out what I took to have been a very deep sigh. Then there was still more silence. Finally, I asked, "Mike?"

"Yeah. I'm here. I'm still trying to decide if I should hang up. I don't think I can legally do that. So speaking, of course, only hypothetically, that's not such an easy question to answer. The strict technical answer would depend on things like who found the body. What was the victim's citizenship? What was the citizenship of the person who found the body? What jurisdiction was willing to actually *respond* to the situation? Where was the body landed? You know, books have been written about this kind of crap."

"So, where the body is brought to shore would have some bearing on this?" I asked.

"It could," he responded. "Generally, in the absence of other overriding factors, the law-enforcement organization closest to where the body is landed will assume initial responsibility for the investigation."

"You want a body?" I asked.

"Speaking hypothetically?" he inquired.

"No."

"Where are you?" he asked.

"We're coming through Redfish Pass," I replied.

"We'll meet you at the county dock south of the causeway."

"Got ya. Be there in about twenty minutes. We'll be in a white, twenty-seven-foot Shamrock."

As we headed down the sound, I reflected on my relationship with Lieutenant Collins—at least, I assumed he was still a lieutenant. For all I knew, he'd been promoted to captain or major or something else by this time. Lord knows he'd gotten enough notoriety, and credit, for having solved the previous murder cases in which our paths had crossed. There'd been the high-profile island resident who'd blown his brains out rather than have to face justice and the wealthy investor who'd almost, with the assistance of an island full of goons, killed Kenny, me, and several of our friends. And, most recently, Jill and I had nearly been burned to death by one of our neighbors as he tried to avoid having to take responsibility for his actions. It's true that, in all these cases, I'd gone out of my way to avoid being publicly recognized as having played any role in helping to bring the culprits to justice. But it's also equally true that without our bumbling interference into his investigations, Collins might never have been able to solve any of these crimes. These cases, of course, could have—indeed perhaps *should* have—ended far differently, with the embarrassed sheriff's department having to issue an explanation for why it had been unable to prevent the deaths of a group of amateur island vigilantes. Consequently, I could understand completely why Mike Collins would never want to hear from me again. Despite this history, I had a lot of respect for him. And I hoped that he might, although he'd never admit it, have some for me, too. In any case, I knew he'd most likely have some smart-ass comment for me when we met at the county dock.

"What did Collins have to say?" asked Kenny, having come to from his lengthy slumber.

"He asked me to pass along to you his warmest regards," I said.

"Like hell he did. Did he say we did the right thing to bring R. V. to him?" Kenny inquired.

"Yeah. When we were speaking hypothetically, that seemed like as good an outcome as any," I replied.

"How about when you weren't speaking hypothetically?" asked Kenny.

"I got the impression that he might have been happier if we'd just left R. V. where we found him," I said.

"Really?" asked Kenny.

"Well, he wasn't exactly overjoyed to hear from us again, but at the same time, he didn't really have much choice," I replied.

"Yeah. I can see that," said Kenny. "So he knows I'm with you?"

"No. I didn't mention that."

"So I could jump ship, and he wouldn't be the wiser?"

"If that's what you want to do," I replied.

I could see Kenny mulling the thought over in his head.

He finally said, "Nah. I couldn't do that. Even if I could swim to shore, there's no way I'd want to miss all the fun."

I laughed at that and said, "Let's just hope there's not as much fun with this one as we had with the last couple of murders we had to deal with."

He laughed and replied, "Let's hope."

***

At idle speed, Rucker steered his boat carefully under the C span of the Sanibel Causeway. To avoid having to deal with boating traffic, he elected to go under the bridge three sets of pilings west of the channel. We all knew there was still more than twenty feet of water in that area and that the clearance overhead was more than ample for Rucker's boat.

As soon as we were clear of the bridge, he turned to the west and began the approach the county dock. We could see the sheriff's department was already on the scene.

As we approached, the first thing I noticed was a dark, mean-looking rigid inflatable boat calmly idling, despite the three three-hundred and fifty horsepower outboards hanging off its stern, about a hundred yards offshore. Its piercing blue strobes warned boaters to stay away. There was also a squad car blocking the entrance road to the dock, its blue iridescent flashers advising anyone who wanted to launch a boat that he or she would need to find another ramp. Several other squad cars were parked near the piers, their strobes sending out additional warnings. An ambulance, thankfully without its red lights flashing, was backed up to the base of the southernmost dock, with bored-looking white-coated attendants standing beside an empty gurney, waiting to be put into action. Parked near the ambulance was a white Ford SUV; its darkly tinted windows, plain-Jane hubcaps, and cowcatcher front bumper unmistakably marked this as a cop's car. I assumed this was Collins's new ride. As I looked toward the end of the dock, I could see him casually leaning against a piling, his weight resting comfortably on one foot. Several other men, whom I took to be deputies, were attentively standing about twenty feet away. When we neared the dock, I observed that Collins's darkly shaded eyes appeared to be staring into the water, probably looking for snook. As Rucker slowed the boat to approach the wharf, Collins's gaze moved to focus instead on us. As the boat gently settled against the pier, he welcomed us with a modest wave and a nod. We returned the gestures.

Kenny was on the bow with a dock line. I was at the stern. Rucker expertly brought the craft to a gentle stop alongside the quay, having to use only the slightest application of the bow thruster to align his boat with the dock. Two deputies were waiting to take the lines from us. I was pleased to note that they tied the lines off to the cleats using proper cleat hitches. They took a couple of other lines from us to use as spring lines. No talking— just good seamanship.

Mike Collins continued to lean against the piling while the boat was secured, not saying a word. I knew that, behind the shades, his eyes were busily absorbing the details of the scene. Finally, after the boat's engine had been shut down, he spoke.

"Damn, Jim, the least you could have done would have been to warn me that Kenny was involved in this one, too. That way I'd have had a chance to try to reassign the case to someone else. Or, maybe, even better, to turn in my resignation. But, hell, it's too late for that now. Who's driving the boat?"

"That's Rucker. This is his boat. We were out grouper fishing. And, oh, by the way, it's good to see you, too."

"Yeah, right! You and Kenny are kind of like my worst night-mares. Y'all just keep coming back, time after time—"

With this, Kenny interrupted, "Lieutenant Collins, my favorite gumshoe. Hope we didn't pull you out here before your dough-nuts were ready."

"Not a chance, Kenny. Not a chance. But I'm surprised you would say something that crude and tasteless. I would have thought a man of your experience would have known that a per-son in my exalted position always has the doughnut shops make deliveries. How're you doing, Kenny?"

"I was doing fine when we were catching grouper, but not so good after I snagged this thing." As he said that, he glanced in the direction of the lump partially covered under a raincoat on the boat's deck.

"Yeah, I can imagine," said Lieutenant Collins. "So y'all caught some grouper?"

"Yep. We were doing pretty good until, well…until we got dis-tracted. We've got a pretty good mess of fish in the icebox."

"Did y'all put some ice on the body?"

"Oh, hell, no!" Kenny said. "We didn't want to take a chance on having the fish go bad. And, besides, I don't think a little ice would have made much difference to him."

After that not quite convivial exchange, Collins turned to Rucker and said, "I must apologize for not having introduced myself earlier, but I trust you can understand how distracting it can be when you have to deal with Pine Island's local riffraff. My name's Mike Collins. And you are Rucker...?"

"Rucker Rasmussen."

"Are you from Saint James City, too?"

"Part of the year. The rest of the time, we live in Ohio."

"I don't blame you. I wouldn't want to spend all year around these two guys, either. Nice boat you've got. It's a vintage Shamrock, isn't it?"

"Yes, it is. I'm impressed you would know that."

"Well, don't be. The only reason I know that is because an uncle of mine has one just like it. He's in the process of restoring it, and sometimes, when I'm not too busy eating doughnuts, I give him a hand," he said, glancing at Kenny.

"Actually," Rucker said, "I restored this boat myself. Took it all the way down to the hull and refinished everything. New engine, new wiring, new plumbing, new through hulls, new paint, new trim, the works."

"Nice job. I'm impressed, but I do need to caution you about something."

"What's that?" Rucker asked.

"I feel it's my duty as a member of Lee County's law-enforcement community to warn you about hanging out with these two undesirables. From my experience, nothing good will come of that."

"Duly noted," Rucker replied.

"Now. Who wants to tell me what we've got here?"

I volunteered that I'd start and Kenny and Rucker would fill in anything I left out.

"We were fifty miles out in the gulf, due west of Redfish Pass. Rucker can give you the exact coordinates off the GPS. We were fishing on some numbers Rucker bought off a guy last week. We had a hell of a bite for a while and finally decided to take a break to drink a beer and let our arms rest. Rucker and I were inside looking at the sonar when Kenny saw something in the water. At first, we didn't know what it was, but we wanted to try to fish it out. Hell, for all we knew, it might have been a bundle of dope." I stopped speaking to see what kind of reaction that statement would engender from the Lieutenant. I wasn't to be disappointed.

"Too bad it wasn't," he said sarcastically. "If y'all had brought that in, the townsfolk would probably have elected y'all honorary mayors of the town, and you'd never have had to buy your own drinks again. Keep going."

"Well, this thing was floating about six to eight feet deep, but eventually, Kenny was able to get a gaff hook in it, and he and Rucker were able to work it to the surface. We weren't happy when we saw what it was; I can tell you that. We thought about just leaving it out there but finally decided that wouldn't be the right thing to do. Then we had to decide who to contact and who to take it to. We didn't really know the legalities of the situation, but we decided we'd just bring it to you and let you deal with whatever would need to be dealt with."

"I hope you don't expect me to thank you," Collins said.

"Nope. We would never expect that from you," I replied with a twinkle in my eye.

"So, is that all there is? Or is there more?"

"Unfortunately, there's more," I replied. "First, all of us know the victim. He's a fellow who goes by the name of R. V. Dodge. He's a resident of, and homeowner in, Saint James City. Supposedly, he's also one of the largest landowners and farmers in Hendry County. Lots of money. His wife lives in town, too."

"What else can you tell me?" Collins asked.

"It looked to us like someone bashed in his skull. And then, we assume, whoever killed him mutilated him. From what we could tell, it looked like someone cut his pecker off, then sewed his lips shut using a grouper rig. And we suspect, but can't confirm, that you may find the missing portion of his genitalia inside his mouth."

"Jesus Christ! What is it with you guys? Why can't you ever dredge up a simple suicide or something that will be easy to solve? No! Not you guys. With y'all, it's always some damn convoluted weirdo frickin' mess that the tabloids and talk shows will love. Wait until the sheriff hears about this one! I knew I should have taken the day off. But y'all do know the guy, huh? What can you tell me about him?"

At that, Kenny spoke up, "He's an asshole!"

"You got anything to say that might further expand on that assessment, Kenny?" Collins asked.

"Nope."

"How about you, Rucker?" the investigator inquired. "What do you know about Mr. Dodge?"

"He had a loud mouth," he answered.

"Anything else you can tell me?"

"Nope."

"And how about you, Jim?"

"He was screwing around on his wife."

Collins didn't say anything. Instead, he just gazed in our direction, his mouth hanging half-open, with what could only be described as a puzzled expression. He focused on Kenny and opened his mouth, as if he were going to speak. But he didn't. Instead, he shifted his attention to Rucker and seemed to go through the same process, a process that ended with the same outcome. Finally, I could see him clench his jaw and take a deep breath, as if steeling himself to make a greater effort. He turned to face me and opened his mouth to ask a question, but then he apparently thought better of that course of action, too. Instead, he just spoke to the deputies on the dock, saying, "Let's get this mess cleaned up. Call the EMTs over, and y'all lift this guy out of the boat and get him on the way to the morgue."

Then, he turned back toward us, looking, I thought, either decidedly tired or defeated, and said, "We'll get him out of here, and then y'all can be on your way. I'll come out to the island tomorrow and take statements from each of you. And, by the way, I do appreciate your assistance. Now, while the guys are doing their jobs, how about if y'all step out of the boat to give them some room?"

Kenny spoke up, "Can we take some beer with us while we wait?"

I could see Collins's jaws tighten and noticed him quickly and automatically glance in the direction of the Lee County sign fastened to the nearby piling that clearly stated "The consumption of alcoholic beverages is strictly prohibited."

Therefore, I was a little surprised when Collins shook his head and said to Kenny, "Sure. Why not? You guys look like you could use one."

"Thanks, Mike," I said. "We'll be down at the end of the dock if you need us."

Rucker and I took our beers and sat on the end of the dock facing the channel, our legs hanging over the edge. Kenny, in his customary manner, paced along one side of the dock and then the other, and looked to see if he could spot a snook hiding behind a piling.

Rucker looked at me and said, "Jim, this has been a heck of a day."

I said, "It's not over yet. We've still got to clean the fish, and I don't know if we're supposed to tell the girls about this or not. I'd sure hate for R. V.'s wife to hear about this through the grapevine. I don't know what the protocol is for notifying her. I guess that's something we'll need to ask Collins about."

While we were talking, we watched as the deputies and EMTs maneuvered R. V. onto a flat stretcher, then lifted him out of the boat and onto a gurney. It didn't take them long. I guessed that this was far from the first time they'd had to deal with handling human remains. As they began to wheel the body toward the ambulance, I approached Mike Collins.

"Mike, if you don't mind my asking, what's the protocol for notifying R. V.'s wife?"

"Unfortunately," he said, "that's my job. And, without question, having to do that is the worst part of this job. Do you know her?"

"Not really. I think her name is Shirley. Jill has some friends who know her real well. I'm sure they'd be glad to help you in any way you might want them to."

"Yeah. I appreciate that, but this is something I have to do personally. That way, not only can I ensure it's done properly, but I also get to observe how the news is received. That's the second-worst part of my job—at this point in an investigation, everyone's a suspect, including you guys."

"Thanks," I said. "So I guess we need to keep this quiet until after you've met with Shirley?"

"Yeah. That would be best. You don't happen to have her phone number, do you?"

"No, but I'm sure I can get it from Jill. You want me to do that?"

"Please. But first ask your friends to keep this quiet for a while."

"OK, Mike. No problem."

I quickly spoke to Kenny and Rucker, and they agreed not to say anything about this until we got the all clear from Collins.

Then I called Jill.

"Hey, babe!" I said when she answered.

"Hello," she drawled in reply. "Are y'all back already?"

"Almost," I said. "We're over by Sanibel, and we'll be home shortly. Then we've got some fish to clean. But right now, I need to ask you a question."

"What do you need?" she asked.

"We ran into a guy who wants to get in touch with Shirley Dodge. Do you have her phone number?"

"Sure. Who wants it?"

"Just a guy Kenny and I know. We were just talking with him, and he said he needed to get in touch with Shirley. I think he wants to ask if he can come over and talk with her about something."

"Jim?"

"Look, babe," I said, "I really can't tell you any more right now, but this is important. Can you please just give me her number? I'll tell you all about this when I get home. And, one more thing, you've got to keep this quiet. You can't tell *anybody* about any of this until I tell you that you can."

"This guy wouldn't happen to be Mike Collins, would he?" she asked.

I didn't answer immediately, trying to decide how best to deal with her inquiry. That delay by itself was apparently enough of an answer for her.

"Damn! Damn! Damn! Not again!" she exclaimed.

"Have you got the number?" I answered.

She gave me the number, before adding, "Your guy can call her, but I don't think he'll be able to go over and see her."

"Why not?" I asked.

"Because," Jill said, "Georgia told me a couple of nights ago that Shirley was in Ohio visiting some friends. She said she'd been there for a few days and was planning to be up there until the end of the week."

"That's interesting," I said. "I'll make sure I tell my guy. Now, remember, don't say anything about this until I tell you that you can. We'll be back on the island in just a little while."

"OK," she replied. "Jim, y'all be careful."

"Yeah. We will. Love you."

"Love you, too," she replied, before clicking off.

After saying good-bye, I typed the phone number into my phone's contacts before I could forget it, then walked over and told Collins what I'd learned. He just nodded as he typed the number into his phone.

As soon as he'd finished typing, he said, "I'll text you as soon as I've been able to talk with her. In the meantime, I'd appreciate it if y'all would keep this quiet."

"Sure," I relied. "Can we take off now?"

"Yeah, but don't forget, I'll be over in the morning to get detailed statements from each of you. Now, get in the boat, and I'll untie your lines."

We were halfway to Saint James City when I heard my phone ding, an indication that I had received a text. I dug the phone from my pocket and read, "Have spoken with Mrs. Dodge. See you at 10:00 a.m.—Collins."

I relayed the message to Kenny and Rucker. They both immediately pulled out their phones to, I presumed, call home. I did the same.

Chapter Fifteen

Saint James City is, in fact, a remarkable little town. While it is partially a boating and fishing village, and partially a place where mainland folks like to go to party, it is, at its core, a simple, unpretentious, unplanned, largely unregulated, semitropical, waterfront community that a few full-time residents are lucky enough to call home. It's surrounded on three sides by water, which helps to ensure that residents enjoy a nearly constant breeze. The village's placement at the southern end of the island overlooks one of Southwest Florida's busiest pleasure-boating thoroughfares, where just a few hundred yards south of town, the Intracoastal Waterway splits, allowing mariners transiting to Florida's east coast the choice of using either the gulf or the passageway through Lake Okeechobee to make that journey. Consequently, it's quite common at any time of the day to hear the usually pleasing sound of a marine engine pushing some type of craft out on the bay.

The homes of the town are clustered along the dozens of canals around which, over time, the village has grown. The houses of the town are a haphazard conglomeration of one-level concrete-block structures, mostly dating from the second half of the last century; two- and three-story stilt homes of various vintages; a scattering of now more or less permanently embedded, but slowly dissolving, mobile homes; and a few modern McMansions haphazardly sprouting like randomly growing weeds. It's a quirky kind of place. And it's certainly not for everyone. But I really like living here.

There are many things about living in Saint James City that I find appealing, but three of the factors I most constantly take pleasure in are our weather, the tropical foliage that grows in this climate, and the large and varied populations of both resident and migratory birds (I'm not talking about the human variety) that call our island home. One of my favorite activities, and I'm using that term very loosely, is to sit beside the pool while watching the leaves of the various types of surrounding palms dip, flutter, and shimmer in the gentle wind blowing across the island. Then, after admiring the twinkling reflections from the canal's ripples, I close my eyes and listen as various avian dialogues penetrate the soothing white-noise hum of palm fronds in motion.

That's what I was doing this morning as I awaited Lieutenant Collins's visit. My eyes were closed, and my head was tilted to one side, resting pleasurably in my right hand. At that particular moment, my aural focus was on what sounded like an irritated, persistent cheeping coming from an osprey located somewhere across the canal. Occasionally, that distinctive call would be superseded by ringing tinkles from Jill's wind chime that hangs on the front porch, or by the clanking noise from the canal-side flag's halyard hardware as it bounced lightly against the metal pole. I was in a deep reverie, enjoying this almost symphonic melody when I was disturbed by an intrusive knocking on the metal frame of the pool's screen door. Knowing who it was likely to be, I kept my eyes closed for a few moments longer than necessary, savoring the morning's delights while taking in one last long, deep breath of fresh morning air. Then I opened my eyes and turned to see the amused, but somehow still scowling, face of Mike Collins.

"Damn, Story," he said. "I thought you were the early-riser type, you being an ex-banker and all that. I wouldn't expect you to be taking a nap in the middle of the morning. May I come in?"

"Sure, Mike," I said. "Come on in, and I wasn't sleeping. I was listening to…oh, shit. Just forget about it. You want some coffee?"

"I'd love a cup, but—"

"Don't start that crap," I interrupted. "Jill's not here. She's gone to the beauty shop, but you don't have to worry about me making the coffee. It'll be coming from a K-Cup."

"Well, in that case, I'll take a cup. Make it black and strong."

"Have a seat. I'll be right back."

I was gone only three, maybe four at the most, minutes. When I returned with a steaming, fragrant cup of concentrated, darkly roasted Bustello-brand coffee, I was surprised to find Collins sitting with his eyes closed, purring softly, looking much the same as I likely had a few minutes earlier. I didn't want to wake him, but I decided to place the coffee down on the table with perhaps a little more force and noise than I otherwise might have. That did the trick. The lieutenant's head jerked, and his eyes popped open.

"Here's your coffee, Mike," I said. "Were you listening to the birds, too?"

"Screw the dang birds! And screw you, too," he growled. "I was chasing some damn kid all over Sanibel Island just about all night. We finally got him a little after three thirty when he drove his car into a palm tree. So, no, I wasn't listening to the birds. I was taking a nap. Please, tell me that isn't decaf."

"Nope. It's good Cuban-style Bustello. It should do the trick."

"Great. That's precisely what I need."

I didn't say anything, giving him time to enjoy and benefit from the coffee. Besides, it was his meeting. Finally, after he'd consumed a third of the cup, he spoke.

"Jim, this is an official interrogation. You should consider yourself to be under oath, and I have to warn you that anything you say may, and will, be used against you in a court of law."

"Fair enough," I replied. "But before we get to all that crap, you said yesterday that you had been able to contact Shirley Dodge?"

"Yes. I spoke to her right after you guys left."

"If you don't mind my asking, how'd that go?"

"About as you'd expect. She was, of course, upset."

"That part of your job," I said, "can't be fun."

"You're right about that. I absolutely hate having to break that kind of news to someone. It never gets any easier."

"I can only imagine," I replied. "So, is she going to be heading back this way soon? The girls wanted me to ask. They'd like to do whatever they can when she returns to help her get through this."

"Yeah. I suspect she's going to need some help, for sure. Has she got any family here on the island?" Collins asked.

"Not that I know of," I said. "But I do think they've got relatives over in Hendry County."

"Well, that's good. She told me when we spoke that she'd try to get a flight in this afternoon."

"Thanks. I'll let Jill know. Now, let's get back to where you started this conversation. I've got nothing to hide, so what would you like to know?"

"Let's start with how well you knew R. V. Dodge."

"Well enough to speak," I said. "But that's about it. I doubt we've ever said more than fifty words in total to each other."

"What do you know about him?" he asked next.

"He's supposed to be a big farmer over in Hendry County. Tomatoes and watermelons—that kind of stuff. Supposedly, he makes a hell of a lot of money. Owns a lot of land, from what I've been told, although I think he inherited most of it from his father. He's got, or at least he had, a very big mouth and an extremely loud voice."

"You have any idea about who might have wanted to kill him?" Collins inquired.

I started to open my mouth to say no, but before anything could come out, I shut it, reflecting on some of the things I'd recently heard and trying to decide if I should share them with Lieutenant Collins. Eventually, I concluded that there was no good reason not to tell him everything I knew.

"Actually," I said, "I can think of at least three, maybe four, people who might have had it in for him."

"Oh, good!" Collins enthused drolly. "That's certainly an improvement over where you and I have started our investigations in the past. So, who do you suspect might have wanted to knock off our vociferous Mr. Dodge?"

"Well, as much as I hate to say it, you'd better put Mack Emory at the top of the list. From what I've been told, he learned recently, from a picture sent to him by Mrs. Dodge, that his wife, Lois Anne, had been, shall we say, sharing her favors with R. V. From what I've been told, as soon as he learned about this, he moved out of the house and quickly decamped to Labelle, the same town R. V. supposedly went to when he was ordered out of *his* house by Mrs. Dodge."

"Actually," Collins said, "that sounds to me like two suspects: Mack Emory and Shirley Dodge."

"Yep," I agreed. "I don't know Mack all that well, but he seems like a nice guy to me. And I don't see how Mrs. Dodge could have done it if she was in Ohio."

"I guess that's where I come in," Collins replied.

"Of course," I said, "but if you don't mind my asking, how long do you think R. V. had been in the water? From the look of things, I'd guess it couldn't have been long."

"Well," Collins answered, "I'll have to wait on the medical examiner for an official answer to that question, but from the fact that nothing had started to chew on Mr. Dodge, I'd guess it could only have been, at the most, a couple of hours. Are you sure y'all didn't see any other boats while you were out there?"

"Not a one," I replied.

"Probably for the best," Collins replied. "Otherwise, you could have stumbled into the middle of something."

"Yeah, I guess. On the other hand, possibly we could have prevented R. V. from being killed," I said.

"Maybe," Collins said. "Now who else do you think might have had it in for R. V.?"

"This is just hearsay, but Kenny told me one of R. V.'s neighbors is an ardent environmentalist. According to Kenny, R. V. and this lady have gotten into several court cases over things she objected to R. V. having done in the neighborhood."

I filled Collins in with the particulars about the squabbles and settlements concerning the mangroves and the retention pond and continued with a description of their recent confrontation over the eagle and the drone.

"Sounds like our boy, R. V., was not exactly an environmentally sensitive kind of guy," Collins said. "Do you know this lady's name?"

"I think it's Adrienne or something like that. She lives right next door to the Dodges, on the west side, I believe."

"She'll be easy enough to find," Collins said.

"Would think so," I agreed. "Especially since she's likely already having a big party to celebrate her dearly beloved neighbor's recent demise."

"Anyone else I ought to look into?" Collins asked.

"No. Not really," I said.

"What's 'not really' mean?" asked Collins.

"Well, I know there can't be anything to this, but I overheard recently that Kenny had nearly gotten into a fight with R. V. down at Froggy's, and that Kenny, apparently, told R. V. he was going to kill him."

Collins stared into my eyes for a moment before shaking his head and quietly muttering, "Pine Island!"

Chapter Sixteen

Jill returned a few hours later. I complimented her on how great her new hairstyle looked, to which she replied, rather coolly I thought, that she'd had only a pedicure. Of course, I responded that her nails looked great, too.

"So glad you noticed," she replied. "How'd your meeting with Mike Collins go?"

"Good, I guess. He just wanted to know if I could think of anyone who might have wanted to kill R. V."

"What'd you tell him?" she asked.

I told her what I'd told Lieutenant Collins.

"You told him you thought Kenny might have killed him?"

"No, of course not. I just told him I'd heard that Kenny had threatened to kill R. V. That's not quite the same thing," I said.

"I guess not," she replied. "Did you tell Kenny you'd told that to Collins?"

"No. I didn't see any reason to do that. I'm sure Kenny will tell him the same thing. And, besides, I've promised myself that this time I am not going to get involved in another investigation."

"I'm glad to hear that," Jill responded. "Did Mike say how Shirley Dodge had taken the news?"

"Not well," I replied. "He said she was pretty upset."

"I bet," Jill said. "That had to be a shock. Did he say when she was coming home?"

"He told me she was flying in this afternoon."

"I'm glad you found that out. The girls and I want to do whatever we can to help her get through this. This is going to be tough on her. She and R. V. had been together since high school. Actually, I think they'd been sweet on each other since grade school. I'll let Georgia know Shirley's coming home today, and we'll decide what we can do to help her."

With that, she pulled her phone out of her purse, stepped out onto the screened deck, sat down in a rocker, and began typing a text. Shortly thereafter, I could hear the sound of smartphone chimes as the girls jointly formulated their plans for rendering assistance.

In turn, I strolled into the kitchen and made myself a cup of tea. When that was ready, I walked into the living room, sat down in my recliner, and clicked on an afternoon television show. I was determined to not get involved in this investigation in any way. If the girls wanted to comfort Shirley Dodge, that was fine with me, but I was not going to lift a finger to help find out who had killed her husband. I'd learned my lesson.

Later that afternoon, I noticed Jill hard at work in the kitchen. I assumed, logically enough, I thought, that she was preparing our meal for the evening. But when I walked in the kitchen to see what was on the menu, I was taken aback to learn that the casserole she was preparing was for not for me; rather, it was for Shirley Dodge.

The girls, I learned, had decided to fix a meal for Mrs. Dodge, and they were planning to share it with her that evening.

"Going to be anything to eat here?" I asked a little apprehensively.

"Jim, you're a grown man. I'm sure you can find something here somewhere. Look around. Right now I've got more important things to worry about; a lady has just lost her husband, and she needs our help."

"OK, OK," I replied, attempting to spread some oil on the waters I had stirred up inadvertently. "Not a big deal. I'm sure I can find something. So all of y'all are going to visit with her tonight?"

"Yeah. Georgia spoke with Shirley Dodge a little earlier to let her know we were thinking of her and to ask what we might be able to do. Shirley thanked her and asked if we could all come over tonight for a while. She said she really didn't want to be alone in that big house tonight. I can understand that. She and R. V. had spent their entire adult lives together. I can't imagine what she must be going through now."

"I can't, either," I replied. "So what are y'all taking over for dinner?"

"I'm bringing this chicken casserole. Janice is taking roasted potatoes. Gigi is making her beet and goat cheese salad. Carolyn is bringing baked asparagus. Sarah is baking her famous chicken and bacon appetizers. Roxie is bringing a shrimp cocktail, and Laura is doing dessert. Georgia is responsible for the wine."

"Sounds great," I said. "I'm sure Shirley will appreciate y'all doing this for her. One of the best ways for dealing with grief is to have friends around."

"Well, I've never been much of a friend to her, but that was primarily because I didn't want to be around R. V. I feel bad about that now. Shirley, I think, actually is a nice person. I'm happy Georgia was able to set this up, so we can show her some support."

"It is good of y'all to do this. What time do you think you'll be home?"

"I don't know. We'll just have to play it by ear. She might break down as soon as we get there and want to be alone after all. Or she might want us to stay a long time. We just want to be there for her. You probably shouldn't plan to wait up for me."

"OK, babe. If y'all need anything, let me know."

Despite Jill's instructions to the contrary, I stayed awake past my normal ten o'clock curfew. Well past eleven, when I was into watching a sixth consecutive episode of *Mysteries at the... Something or Other*, I heard the garage door open, signaling Jill's return. As I heard the door open, I didn't bother to get up to welcome her, giving her instead what I thought was a sufficiently warm verbal hello. After all, I was really into the story being discussed on TV at that particular moment. In retrospect, I probably should have paid more attention to her arrival. If I had, perhaps I would have been better prepared to deal with what happened next.

It took me a few seconds to focus on the fact that I'd gotten no response to my welcome-home greeting and a few seconds longer to process the significance of that. Only then did I turn to look. I anticipated seeing Jill, probably silently putting something away. What I certainly did *not* anticipate seeing was Jill, Janice, and Gigi all standing side by side behind the couch, arms crossed, animating an unmistakable display of unsympathetic body language. All three were glaring straight at me with eyes that somehow managed to simultaneously convey anger, contempt, pity, and a general desire to knock the stew out of me.

"Well, hello, ladies!" I began, hoping against hope that I'd possibly misread the hostility of the situation. Unfortunately, I had not.

"Jim Story," Jill shouted. "You are an asshole!"

"Whoa, babe," I replied, in what I hoped was my most innocent manner. "What did I do?"

"You, Mister Big Mouth Big Shot, got Kenny arrested. That's what you've done!"

"Huh?" I replied, dazed by what seemed like an incomprehensible accusation.

That's when Janice, Kenny's wife, fired her salvo at me. "Jim, how could you do this? I thought you were Kenny's friend. But no—instead, you threw him under the bus by telling Mike Collins you thought he'd murdered R. V. Dodge! Now he's in jail on charges of obstruction of justice, giving false statements to a law-enforcement officer, bribery, and resisting arrest. And it's all because of you. Some friend *you* are!"

Then Gigi, Janice's sister, said, "Yeah, and they're probably going to also charge him with R. V.'s murder, once they can tie up some loose ends. Of course, if it wasn't so serious, and probably so expensive, I'd think it's funny as hell that my always 'yanking my chain' brother-in-law is in jail. But this is serious, and it is your fault, Jim. Thanks a lot."

"Wait just a damn minute," I said. "Will someone please tell me what's going on?"

"Duh! We just did," Jill said. "I've never been so mad at you. I can't believe you caused all this to happen, and I've never been so embarrassed. As we were leaving Shirley's house, Janice and Gigi pulled me aside. Janice had just gotten a call from Kenny *from the jail* telling her what had happened. I am completely mortified!"

Slowly, as the girls continued to talk, I'd started to piece together what must have gone down. When Kenny had first been interviewed by Mike Collins, he must have never said he'd threatened to kill R. V. Dodge. Possibly he'd even claimed he and R. V. were friends. Then, after Collins had interviewed some of the others, the truth must have started to come out. Collins probably came back to talk to Kenny again and accused him of trying to mislead him. By this time, Kenny likely had been drinking, and who knows what could have gone down then?

"Kenny didn't lie to the police, did he?" I asked Janice.

"At this point, I don't know what he did. But this could have all been avoided if you'd just had the courtesy to let Kenny know you'd told Lieutenant Collins about his run-in with R. V. That's the least you could have done, Jim. I thought you were his friend. I'm sure he never would have imagined that you would tell Mike Collins about what happened at Froggy's."

"Well," I answered, "why would I ever think Kenny wouldn't tell the truth to the sheriff?"

"Maybe," Jill said sarcastically, "he didn't want to get involved, either."

I watched with my mouth hanging open as all three of them stormed out the kitchen door. Ten minutes later, Jill came back in, but she didn't speak. Instead, she marched directly upstairs to our bedroom, making a point to not acknowledge in the least my presence. That was when, as I listened to closet doors and dresser drawers banging shut, I made the decision to sleep downstairs in the spare bedroom.

Chapter Seventeen

The next morning, I didn't wait for Jill to make an appearance. Rather, as soon as the sun was up, I called Mike Collins.

"Good morning, Jim," Collins answered pleasantly.

I was surprised at the amiable nature of his response. In the past, on the few occasions I'd called Mike at this hour, he'd been anything but agreeable. That alone should have alerted me that something was up, but, of course, I'm not that smart.

"Good morning, Mike," I began. "I understand you arrested Kenny."

I waited for him to reply. He said nothing.

"Mike, are you there?"

"I can hear you fine, Story."

Then, again, nothing.

"Mike," I began again, "did you really have to arrest Kenny?"

"Yep."

Then, silence.

"Well, Mike, you do know that Kenny wouldn't have killed R. V.?"

"Nope."

"Damn it, Mike. Kenny couldn't have killed R. V. He was with me fishing that morning."

"Maybe y'all did it together. You were in the vicinity, and Kenny, as we both know, had a motive."

"Mike, come on. You know better than that. We'd never do anything like that."

"That's what they all say, Jim."

"Mike," I whined. "You can't really think we'd do something like that!"

"Relax, Story. At this point, I don't think you, or your two friends, had anything to do with the murder. Hell, if y'all had killed him, I don't think you'd have gone to the effort of dragging his body back in and dumping him on my lap."

"So why do you have Kenny in jail?"

"For starters, he failed to answer my inquiries truthfully. Then, when I called him on that, he got all hot and bothered and told me I was acting like an asshole. When I told him I could arrest him for that, he casually strolled into the living room, sat down in his recliner, started to defiantly sip his scotch, and informed me he certainly wasn't going to go anywhere. I think I can get a judge to interpret that action as resisting arrest."

"So, what'd he really do to piss you off? Did he not offer you a drink?"

"Actually, he did. And I believe that definitely constitutes a clear attempt to bribe an officer of the law."

"Mike! You can't be serious about all this!"

Finally, much to my relief, Collins started to laugh. "Jim, actually, I did have more than enough justification to haul Kenny in. Truthfully, I haven't charged Kenny with anything yet, and I probably won't—that is, if he behaved himself last night. Honestly, I took him in as much for my own amusement as anything else."

"Your amusement?" I exclaimed.

"Yeah. As you know, that cocky little troublemaker has gotten under my skin on numerous occasions, and now, well, it's kind of like payback time."

"So, are you going to let him go?"

"Probably."

"Come on, Mike, jail's no place for an old guy with a smart mouth," I said. "He could get hurt, or maybe even raped, or something."

"Don't you worry about that. He actually shared a cell last night with a fellow named Big John Thompson."

"Big John?" I asked worriedly.

"Yeah, John. Obviously, he's a big guy. Weighs in close to four hundred pounds and looks mean as a snake, but he's really a good guy when he's sober. He periodically comes to visit us after he's been drinking and gotten into it with his old lady. You see, his wife is a good Christian lady and all that, and she won't put up with him drinking. So, invariably, if he comes home drunk, they start to fight—and by the way, she really is mean. Eventually, somebody calls us, and we have to go take John out of there. We end up keeping him for a month or so, then she'll drop the charges, and they leave holding hands, hugging and kissing each other. That'll last for about six months."

"So you put Kenny in with Big John so he'd look out for him?" I asked.

"That's one of the reasons," Collins replied. "I did ask John to make sure no one messed with Kenny, and they won't have. You can be sure of that. But I also asked John to try to mess with Kenny just a little."

"You didn't!" I said.

"Yeah, I did." Collins laughed. "I just couldn't help myself. I'm willing to bet Kenny didn't sleep much last night. Hopefully, the experience did him some good, and maybe he'll treat me with a little more respect in the future. But I plan to let him out this morning."

"Well, that's good. I'm sure the ladies will be glad to hear that. Maybe that'll even help me to get out of the doghouse with them."

"Tell you what, Story. I'll tell Kenny I'm only letting him go because you asked me to."

"Please do. I need all the help I can get."

Chapter Eighteen

Jill had not come down yet, so I quietly climbed the stairs to see if she was awake. She wasn't, so I gently lay down alongside her and tenderly snuggled up against her back. I was hoping she'd forgotten about last night.

But, of course, she hadn't.

"Don't you dare touch me," she said. Not exactly the response I had been hoping for.

"OK," I whispered, sliding a few inches away. Then I played my trump card. "I got Mike Collins to release Kenny, and all the charges are going to be dropped."

She sat up straight and said, "Oh, honey, that's wonderful! Thank you, thank you, thank you." She leaned over, gave me a hug and a quick passionate kiss, and said, "I've got to call Janice. This will make her feel so much better."

"Yeah, you should do that," I replied. "I'll be here waiting for you after you do that."

She gave me a wink; I thought that was a very good sign. She then dialed Janice.

"Janice, Jim just told me he asked Mike Collins to let Kenny go, and he agreed. Collins is going to drop all the charges, too. Isn't that great news?"

They carried on for a few minutes longer. Eventually, Jill said good-bye, and then rolled over next to me.

"Janice said to tell you thank you and that she forgives you for what you did to Kenny."

"Forgiven, but not forgotten, huh?" I said.

"Well, you *are* an asshole," she replied.

"Possibly, but at least I'm a lovable one."

"Well, I guess we'll just have to see about that," she replied suggestively.

And that's what we did. Thirty minutes later, after all the heavy breathing was over and our heartbeats had returned to normal, we started to talk.

"You never told me how last night went with Shirley," I said.

"Oh, Jim, at first it was awful. She completely broke down—sobbing, crying, shaking. For a while, she was in a bad way. I was actually worried for her. But, finally, she began to settle down, and I was glad we were there for her. I think she just really needed someone to talk with so she could release the pain and grief she was feeling."

"That's good," I said. "I'm glad y'all went to see her. You were there for quite some time."

"Yeah, after an hour or so, she started to feel better, so we ate dinner and drank the wine Georgia had brought over. I think the meal helped her. After that we drank more wine, and then we just sat around and talked. I think that helped her, too."

"What did y'all talk about?" I asked.

"Basically, we all listened as Shirley remembered the things that she and R. V. had done over the years. She'd talk, and she'd laugh, and she'd cry for a while, and then she'd move on to another story. And soon there'd be more tears and more laughter. And, of course, all of us were laughing and crying along with her."

"It sounds like," I said, "y'all needed a lot of Kleenex."

"Yeah," Jill agreed. "I guess we did go through a couple of boxes. Fortunately, Janice had thought to bring them."

"But," I said, "it sounds like you all got along with her pretty good."

"Yeah, we did. Of course, given the circumstances, we kind of had to. Still, it was good for her, and I think that going forward, the card group is going to include her in some of the stuff we do. She's going to need the company, for sure."

Chapter Nineteen

The rest of the morning passed pleasurably. I spent some time on the pool deck reading. Jill chatted on the phone for a while with one of our daughters, and more importantly with one of our grand-daughters, then puttered around upstairs organizing her closet. As the lunch hour approached, I, in my customarily insensitive manner, tracked her down to ask about our options for lunch.

"You're not hungry *again*?" was her answer.

"Well, it is almost noon," I replied, answering in what to me had seemed like a logical enough manner.

"Jim, don't you know where the kitchen is?"

"Of course I do, babe, but I hate to rummage around in there and mess up your meal plans."

"Oh, don't worry about that, Jim. Feel free to fix whatever you can find."

"Actually, babe," I said, hoping to change the direction and likely outcome of where the conversation was heading, "I was hoping maybe we could go out and I could buy you a nice lunch."

Apparently, that was the right thing for me to have said.

"That sounds like a wonderful idea," she answered. "Do you know who's playing this afternoon down at Ragged Ass?"

"I don't have a clue," I replied. "Who's playing?"

"Ellie Lee and Blues Fury," she answered. "I was hoping maybe we could ride down there on our bicycles, get a table, and have lunch. Maybe we can get some friends to join us, too."

"I like it," I responded. "But we better get going if we expect to get a table."

"Yeah," Jill said. "Why don't you go blow up the bike tires, and I'll text the girls and see who wants to join us."

Ragged Ass Saloon and Grill is one of Saint James City's best-known hangouts. It's essentially a biker bar (with lots of convenient dockage for any boaters who might want to join in)—but in a friendly, respectable sort of way. Apparently, one of some retirees' favorite activities is to act out their Hells Angel fantasies. They quickly acquire a loud, mean-sounding, chopped and customized Harley; obtain an ensemble of biker's leathers and clothing; and join an accommodating motorcycle club. These clubs, of course, need appropriate destinations to which their members, as a group, can ride. That's where the Ragged Ass Saloon comes into play. It's twenty miles or so away from most of the mainland's retirement meccas, far enough for a good day's ride. And it's sufficiently disreputable, both in its name and in its Saint James City canal-side location, to satisfy the fantasies of most of the members and their sissy-bar-supported spouses. Having grown up in the *Easy Rider* era, I can easily understand the fantasy, but in my mind, I tend to associate that culture more with images of a couple of brooding lone-wolf bikers riding down a deserted road, trying to escape the conformity of law-abiding society—rather than with the sight of a convoy of hundreds of similarly attired and similarly transported bikers, traveling together as a group. I guess they must have watched a different biker movie.

Regardless, Saint James City is always glad to have the bikers out on the weekends. They bring good business and help to justify places like Ragged Ass in their hiring good bands to entertain the crowds. And good bands give the locals reason to go to the bars, too, which is why Jill and I were soon pedaling our bikes up Stringfellow Road toward the north end of town. Ellie Lee is the lead guitarist and vocalist for an excellent blues-rock trio based up in Tampa. Periodically she comes down our way to play, and when she's in town, we always try to catch her show. Her covers of Stevie Ray Vaughn, Jimi Hendrix, and the pantheon of other blues-based guitar heroes are not to be missed.

As we coasted off the road and into the parking lot, we were delighted to see we had beaten the iron-horse-riding hordes and thankfully were able to sit down on the benches of an empty family-size picnic table that was strategically located in the shade and had a decent view of the stage. The afternoon was off to a good start.

Jill ordered a pitcher of Mich Ultra for herself, while I (since the place doesn't have a liquor license) started with a wine-based Bloody Mary that tasted surprisingly like the real thing. We also requested a couple of appetizers; we knew we needed to pace ourselves for what was likely to be a long afternoon. The appetizers had just been delivered when Roxie and her companion of the month, Prince, joined us. Not long after that, we saw Georgia and Robert pull into the parking lot in their restored old jeep. We waved them over to the table. Our waitress saw them coming and arrived to take their orders almost as soon as they had sat down. A few minutes later, there were several additional pitchers of beer, a couple of bottles of wine, and another Bloody Mary for me on the table. So much for pacing ourselves. Then, as soon as everyone had drinks in their hands, the conversation started, and it was clear that the island telegraph had been rapidly, if not especially accurately, spreading the news about Kenny's arrest.

"Oh, my God," Roxie said. "I can't believe Kenny has been arrested for killing R. V.!"

"Well, that's actually not—" I began, but I was immediately interrupted by Georgia.

"That's what I heard, too," she said. "I also heard he was drunk and belligerent and resisted arrest. In fact, I heard the cops had to tase him twice just to get him under control enough to put the cuffs on him!"

"No, I don't think—" I started again. This time, Roxie intruded.

"Oh, I hadn't heard that, but I'm not surprised. You know how out of control he can get when he's been drinking too much scotch. I bet that's why he killed R. V., too. You do know he and R. V. got into a huge brawl down at Froggy's. I heard they really broke up the place."

"Now, wait just a dang minute," I began again, speaking more loudly and forcefully. "And this time don't y'all interrupt me. Kenny was released this morning, and the whole thing was just a big misunderstanding. I spoke with Lieutenant Collins this morning and straightened the whole thing out." As I said that, I noticed Jill rolling her eyes.

Then, almost as if on cue, we saw Kenny, Janice, and Gigi drive into the parking lot. Janice was driving their newly acquired golf cart, and Kenny was on the back. From this I deduced that Kenny had already started to celebrate his newly won freedom. We all yelled and waved at them as they pulled the cart in next to a long row of leaned-over, kickstand-supported bikes. My first thought was to hope Kenny wouldn't stumble into one of them as he dismounted. Fortunately, he didn't.

Soon, Kenny was surrounded by ladies hugging and kissing him and, in general, welcoming him back from his adventure in incarceration. It was clear Kenny was enjoying the adulation; the more attention they gave him, the more animated, and the louder, his accounts of the experience became. Soon, other women from the crowd came over to see what all the hoopla was about, and in no time they were buying Kenny beer, and hugging on him, too.

Then, just as the adulation reached a plateau, Ellie began to play, effectively drowning out further conversation with a loud, bluesed-up, emphatic version of "Jailhouse Rock." When she finished singing, she slowly spoke into her mic, emphasizing what she was saying with a somewhat coquettish, come-hither inflection, and dedicated that opening number to Kenny, explaining as she did that he had just been released from Lee County's slammer. She then pointed at Kenny, asked him to stand up, and requested that the crowd give him a round of applause, which they gleefully did. That announcement caused what had already been a full-scale welcome-home celebration to become even more energized. As she finished speaking and began to play again, I looked around our table, wondering how in the heck Ellie had known about Kenny's escapade. That was when I noticed a rather pleased look on Robert's face. Instantly, I understood he had requested the song and the dedication. And, knowing Robert, I knew he would have likely tipped Ellie very well to ensure his wishes were followed. As he turned to look in my direction, I caught his eye, nodded at him, and gave him a thumbs-up to acknowledge a card well played. He laughed. The party continued, with Ellie doing her best to honor Stevie Ray and the other masters of the blues. She was almost through the first set when Shirley Dodge arrived in the parking lot, wheeling the gaudy, chrome-bedecked, stretch golf cart that had been R. V.'s pride and joy. Momentarily, I wondered about the propriety of a grieving widow coming to this kind of party, but I quickly reasoned that in her position, I would probably have done the same thing. It couldn't have been much fun sitting all alone in that big house when everyone else in town was down at the Ragged Ass, grooving to the blues and having fun. Many of the women in the crowd, including all the women at our table, went out to welcome and comfort her. I couldn't help but notice as the girls dragged Shirley over to our table that it looked as if she had been crying. I hoped the music would do her some good.

Ellie, of course, having no idea who Shirley was or what she was going through, continued to work through her normal first set. I was worried when I heard the band begin Albert King's "The Sky is Crying" that this might be too much for Shirley's delicate emotional state. Fortunately, she was so involved in chatting with those trying to comfort her that the song hadn't bothered her at all. Ellie then finished her set with an amped-up, energetic rendition of "Red House," which helped to dissolve any lingering atmospherics of sorrow. She then left the stage for a well-deserved rest. The relative quiet that followed energized the ladies at the table, as they immediately surrounded Shirley and offered even more profuse expressions of compassion.

Shirley, as soon as she found a moment to break free of the throng of ladies offering condolences, turned, took hold of Kenny's arm, and said, "Kenny, I'm so glad they let you out of jail. I knew you couldn't have possibly killed R. V. And, you know, he actually liked you. He just enjoyed picking on you to get you riled up. That was just his way of having fun with you."

"Thank you, Shirley," Kenny said. "I actually liked R. V., too. I'm sorry for your loss."

"Thank you, Kenny," she said. "That was kind."

With that, the ladies once again began to talk, and the guys walked over to stand on top of the seawall that borders the canal. Ostensibly, the reason for our stroll was to stretch our legs, but in truth we really wanted to look at the boats tied up out back. We spent the next few minutes critiquing what we saw, and arguing mildly about which of the vessels we would most like to have. Not for the first time, the thought crossed my mind that men look at boats and women in much the same way. I had just started to let my mind wander down the path of exploring that idea further when Kenny brought us back to reality by pointing out a convoy of sheriff's department cruisers and a crime-scene van driving south on Stringfellow Road. As we watched, we could see it turn left onto Eighth Avenue.

"Thank God they didn't turn on my street!" Kenny exclaimed.

"Oh, hell, Kenny," I said, "they're probably just lost. Maybe I ought to call and give them directions to your house."

"Damn it, Jim. Don't you dare. You've done enough to throw me under the bus already.

"Listen, man, I'm really sorry about what happened. I never thought that Collins would take that so seriously, and besides, I assumed that you would have mentioned the incident to him. Regardless, I wish I'd have given you a heads-up."

"Don't worry about it, Jim. It's what I get for running my mouth. But, I'll tell you one thing—I don't ever want to go back in that jail again."

"How come, Kenny?" I asked, in what I hoped was an innocent enough manner.

"There are a lot of big, bad, and very unhappy people in that place," he said. "If it hadn't been for my cellmate, John, I don't know what might have happened to me!"

"You got along with your cellmate?" I asked, trying to not sound too surprised.

"Yeah, but not at first," Kenny said. "That guy was larger and meaner looking than anyone else in the jail. If he hadn't liked to play dominoes, I don't know what might have happened."

"You played dominoes with him?" I asked incredulously.

"Sure did. Granted, at first he was acting kind of hinky, but once he learned I could play, and play well, he and I became good friends. After that, nobody dared to mess with me."

"Did you get any sleep while you were in there?" I asked.

"Slept like a baby. I snored, Big John snored, and nobody screwed with us."

"Well, that was good," I said. "I wonder where those cops were going."

"Let me call my buddy Pat. He lives down that way. I'll find out if he can see what they're doing." He pulled out his cell and stepped away to make the call. A few minutes later, he was back.

"Well?" I asked.

"Pat says they've surrounded Mack Emory's house with crime-scene tape, and the deputies aren't letting anyone get near it. The guys from the van, dressed in hazmat suits, are inside."

"I wonder what that's about," I said.

"It looks to me like Collins must have someone else in his crosshairs now," Robert said.

"Is Lois Anne still in the house?" I asked.

"No. She left town as soon as Mack moved out," Robert offered. "Georgia told me a friend of hers saw her in Labelle a couple of days ago. I haven't seen her there myself."

"If I had to bet, I'd guess Mack Emory killed R. V.," said Prince. "It seems to me that he's the most obvious suspect."

"Yeah, probably," we all agreed.

When we returned to the table, it was obvious that the girls had gotten some news, too.

"Did y'all hear?" asked Jill. "Roxie just got a call that the sheriff's department is searching Mack Emory's house."

"Yeah, we heard that," I said. "The crime-scene unit is processing his house right now."

At that point, Shirley Dodge started to cry. Georgia put her arm around Shirley's shoulders to comfort her and began to assure her that everything was going to be all right. Shirley wasn't having any of it.

"Y'all don't understand," she wailed. "This is all my fault. If I hadn't sent those awful pictures to Mack, none of this would have happened. R. V. wouldn't be dead, and Mack wouldn't be in trouble. It's all my fault!" At that point she broke down and began to sob loudly.

Everyone at the surrounding tables looked in our direction with concern on their faces, unsure how to help. Even Ellie looked worried, obviously delaying the start of her next set to let the situation resolve itself.

"Come on, Shirley," Georgia said. "I'll take you home with me, and you can rest. We'll keep you company." With that, the ladies all stood up and helped Shirley over to the passenger side of her jeep. "I'll drive," said Georgia. The other three ladies climbed into the back of the vehicle, and away they went. I could see Shirley was still crying, and the others were patting her shoulders in concern. Georgia eased the jeep out of the parking lot, doing her best to be inconspicuous in spite of the irritatingly loud rumble from the vehicle's glass-packed muffler. Nevertheless, almost everyone in the crowd silently watched them leave; it was almost as if they were trying to pay respect at a funeral.

Once the ladies were gone, all the guys looked at one another. Robert spoke first. "All right, what do we do now? And how do I get home?"

"And how do I get Jill's bike home?" I added.

I could see Robert open his mouth to reply, but then, as if he'd reconsidered what he was going to say, he closed it. Prince did the same.

Finally, Kenny made a suggestion on which we could all agree. "I think we're probably going to need to drink on those questions a little bit longer."

"Yep," we all agreed and sat down at our table. Simultaneously, Ellie and the boys drowned out further conversation with the familiar chords of one of Stevie Ray's biggest hits.

Chapter Twenty

I spent the next morning in the yard picking up palm fronds and contemplating how best to remove the coconuts from a tree that towers over the stone walkway leading to my dock. My neighbor had recently told me that more people are killed in Florida by falling coconuts each year than by being struck by lightning. Ever since that conversation, I'd lived in fear that one of these heavy, hard orbs was going to fall on someone's head.

When we'd first moved in, I could easily reach the top of this tree with a polesaw. Then, for the next couple of years, I'd been able to climb a stepladder and use the saw to remove the nuts. Last season, I'd had to resort to purchasing a very tall stepladder, one with a platform on top. Now, even with that impressive addition to my gardening armory, I wasn't quite able to saw the nuts off. I'd just made the decision to pay a professional to deal with the removal of this year's coconuts when I heard the phone ringing inside the house. I figured that, as usual, it would be for Jill. I was wrong.

"Jim, it's Mike Collins," Jill yelled.

"I'll be right there," I replied, wondering why in the heck he was calling me. I walked into the house and picked up the phone.

"Good morning, Mike," I said.

"Morning, Jim. Hope I didn't disturb you."

"Nope. I've been up for hours doing yard work," I replied, exaggerating the truth a bit to prepare the groundwork for my rejoinder. "But isn't it kind of early for you to be doing the people's business, Mike?"

"Yeah, for sure," he replied, deftly batting away my jest. "I was wondering if you might be available for lunch today."

"Sure, I can make it. When and where?"

"Noon, at the Waterfront," he replied.

"See you there."

As soon as I hung up, Jill asked, "So Mike wants you to get involved in this investigation, too?"

"No, of course not. He probably just wants to warn me to stay out of it. There's no reason for me to get involved in this case. I hardly even knew the guy." Then, both to change the subject, and because of genuine concern, I asked, "How was Shirley Dodge last night?"

"Jim, to be honest, I'm not sure. For a while she appeared to be fine, but then somebody would say something innocent enough, and she'd just fall to pieces again."

"Isn't that what people who are grieving do?" I replied.

"Yeah, I guess. That's what I keep telling myself, but still…"

"What are you saying, Jill? Do you think Shirley is faking being upset?"

"No, Jim, of course not! I guess it's just that I never been close to Shirley. I don't know her that well, so, you know, it's kind of hard for me to understand how she's reacting and to keep it all in perspective. I really do feel bad for her. We all do. And I'd hate to be in her shoes. That's for sure."

"Oh, don't give me that, Jill!" I replied, winking as I did, just so she'd know I was teasing. "If somebody had knocked me off, you'd be celebrating, and you know it."

"Yeah," she responded, not missing a beat. "But I'd still hate to have to deal with cleaning out your closet and stuff like that."

"So, you wouldn't miss me at all, baby?" I asked, knowing as I did that I was once again acting as the straight man in the unending comedy skit that has always defined our relationship.

"Probably, but only when I needed someone to carry out the garbage!" she responded. "Now, you'd better get cleaned up if you're going to meet Mike at noon."

"But…"

She was gone.

The Waterfront is one of Saint James City's most respected dining establishments. It operates in a small wooden building that perches next to one of our canals, near where that waterway empties into San Carlos Bay. The building was once the town's original schoolhouse. Inside, to the left, after you come through the heavy wooden, porthole-adorned door, is a bar area. It features a long rustic bar that is fronted with a dozen or so stools, and four high-top, four-seat tables along the facing wall. The main room, looking (with a little imagination) as though it could still serve as an institution of learning for young kids, contains ten tables of varying seating capacities. The ceiling of the room is decorated with crayon artwork that has been scribbled by diners onto what had previously been white butcher-paper table coverings. The vibe of the room is friendly, fun, and neighborly. Outside, after passing through another heavy, porthole-pierced door is a row of benches and tables arranged on a deck facing the canal. When the weather's good, that's where most of the restaurant's action is.

As I came through the main door, one of the waitresses recognized me and pointed me toward the rear door. I went through it and found Collins sitting at the last table on the left. I wasn't really surprised. Not only would this location, at least for a short while, be somewhat private, it would, more importantly, be in the shade of an overhanging tropical tree.

As I walked toward his table, I could see Collins talking on his cell. He saw me coming and waved at me to sit down. I motioned at him to continue his call and stopped out of hearing range to give him time to finish. As I waited, I noticed that he appeared to be looking much less tired than the last time I'd seen him. A minute later, I saw him click off and motion for me to join him.

He extended his right hand, and as I sat down, we shook. "It's good to see you again, Jim," he began. "I appreciate you coming. How's Kenny?"

I laughed. "He's good now. That was certainly a nasty trick you played on him. But you enjoyed playing that card, didn't you?"

"Yeah. That was so much fun. You know, I think having a chance to laugh like that actually may have been good for me. I've been sleeping so much better."

"Well, I'm sure Kenny will be relieved to know he was able to improve your sleep. You're lucky, as far as I'm concerned, that he hasn't tried to sue you. But, actually, he's not upset about it at all. As a matter of fact, he's been milking his short stay in your establishment for all its worth, and he's been getting a lot of free drinks because of it."

"Good! I'm glad he's gotten some benefit from the experience, too. Hopefully, he's learned a lesson."

"I don't know about that," I said. "From the way he tells the story, he enjoyed the adventure and had a lot of fun playing dominoes with Big John."

"Yeah, I didn't count on them bonding like that. At least he didn't get hurt. So, how are you doing? And, more importantly, how's Jill?"

"She's fine, Mike. She asked me to give you her regards."

"Tell her I appreciate that, and please pass mine along as well. You doing OK?"

"Yeah, Mike, I'm fine, but before we go any further, I want you to know that I promise you, and I've promised Jill, that I'm not going to get involved in the Dodge investigation. I didn't know the guy well, and I've got absolutely no reason to stick my nose in it. I want you to know that."

Collins began to reply, but he had to hold what he'd been about to say because of our waitress's arrival. She pleasantly and professionally took our orders and filled our water glasses. As she departed, Lieutenant Collins began again, "Jim, I know this is going to sound kind of strange coming from me, but actually I was hoping that you might, after a fashion, become involved in the case. In fact, the reason I wanted us to have lunch was to try to solicit some of your thoughts on this mess. If, in the past, I had paid more attention to you, I could have saved myself a lot of time and avoided a lot of embarrassment. And, Lord knows, I could have saved myself from having to listen to the sheriff ridicule me, every chance he gets, about how Pine Island's 'Over the Hill Gang' has managed three different times to put one over on his ace senior detective. I've even heard him threaten to put you guys on retainer. Seriously, Jim, the sheriff's up for reelection this year, and he's putting a lot of pressure on me to wrap this thing up as quickly as possible. Look, I know you know this island and the people who live here a heck of a lot better than I do. And, in the past, you and your friends have been able to get to the bottom of what's going on quicker than I have. So, before I, once again, go and do something that I might ultimately regret having done, I thought that I'd straight-up ask for your opinion about who killed R. V. Dodge."

Hearing this, I leaned away from the table, sat up straight, and looked Collins in the eyes. "Damn, Mike, I'm flattered you think so highly of our abilities, but you and I both know we just got lucky before. And, in fact, we were lucky not to get ourselves killed. Speaking for myself, I really don't want anything to do with this case, and I was serious when I said I really didn't know R. V. Dodge. We said hello a couple of times, but that's it."

"I know, Jim," Collins said. "You've told me that already. But, look, here's why I'm asking for your help: I've got enough to arrest Mack Emory. He had motive, opportunity, and the means to do it. He was overheard threatening to kill R. V. And, not only was he upset about R. V. messing with his wife, he was also upset about her having given his grouper numbers to R. V. The sheriff's told me twice that he doesn't understand why I haven't already put the guy in a cell. I'm probably going to have to. But, before I do that, I wanted to get your thoughts one more time on whether you think he could have killed R. V. I know you've been fishing with him, and I've been told you spent the whole day talking with him while you were on his boat."

"Yeah. I did, but it was only that one time. And, honestly, we were just talking about fishing."

"OK. I can buy that, but I still want to know if you think Mack could have killed R. V."

"How the hell am I supposed to know something like that? Look, he seemed like a nice enough guy. Actually, I liked him a lot, but when we were on the boat, he didn't have all that much to say. When he did speak, he seemed like the kind of guy I'd like to be around. He liked the water, handled his boat well, spoke quietly, and knew how to fish. What's not to like? So, if you just want my opinion, he didn't seem like the kind of guy who would kill somebody...but who knows what any man would do if he found out what Mack found out about what his wife had been doing with R. V.? That might have been enough to send him, or anyone, over the edge."

"Yep. I've seen that happen way too many times. But I wanted to get your thoughts about Mack. Actually, that's kind of my opinion about him, too. Unfortunately, as I said a minute ago, all the evidence we've got squarely points in his direction. We know that R. V. was messing around with his wife, we know his wife gave R. V. a chip that contained all of Mack's precious grouper numbers, and we know R. V. shared those numbers with his friends and drinking buddies. Beyond that, I've learned that Mack was responsible for poisoning a couple million dollars' worth of R. V.'s watermelons, and in retaliation, R. V. was suing Mack and had promised to ruin him professionally. It doesn't help that y'all found R. V.'s body floating in the middle of Mack's favorite grouper hole. And, finally, Mack has admitted to being out on his boat, alone, without an alibi, the morning R. V. was killed. I know this is not conclusive, but it's enough. It's more than enough. I'm probably going to have to arrest him, even if I don't feel good about it. I was actually hoping you might be able to talk me out of doing it."

"Sorry," I said. "What about the other suspects? The environmentalist neighbor, for example."

"No dice. She and her husband have been on vacation for the past month touring Maine and the Canadian Maritimes in their motor coach. Plus, they're both in their midseventies. I really can't see them being involved."

"OK," I said. "Maybe another member of the Pine Island EcoMafia could have done it for them."

"EcoMafia?" Lieutenant Collins asked.

"You know there are a lot of us out here who feel pretty strongly about the environment," I said.

"So you might have killed R. V. over the environment?" Collins asked.

"No. Not me," I answered. "My passion is clean water, and R. V. really didn't do much to damage that, but there a lot of others who really love the island's eagles. Perhaps one of them did it because of the drone incident."

"Nah, I don't think so. If you'll excuse the pun, that just seems like a wild-goose chase to me."

"Well, OK. What about Mrs. Dodge? If anyone had a motive, she did."

"Jim, I've verified that Shirley Dodge was in Chicago when R. V. was killed. So she's out."

"You really don't have any other suspects?" I asked.

"Kenny, as we know, was with you. Unless you've got another suggestion, I'm fresh out of possibilities."

"Sorry, Mike. I wish I could be of more help, but you're on your own with this one."

"Yep," Collins replied. "I don't see any other way this could have gone down. I've got to tell you, I don't feel good about it, though."

"Neither do I, Mike. Neither do I."

The food arrived, and we ate a rather quiet, somber meal. As we finished and walked toward Collins's car, I told him, "If I learn or hear anything, I'll let you know."

"I appreciate that, Jim. I'll try to keep you in the loop, too."

"Are you going to arrest Mack?"

"I don't know yet."

I pedaled my bike back to the house. That's another of the perks of living in Saint James City: everything is easily accessible by bicycle. When I walked in, Jill was in the kitchen cleaning bowls and dishes. I could smell something baking in the oven, something that smelled sweet—probably a dessert to be shared with the girls.

As I entered, she looked up from what she was doing and said, "Hi, babe. How was lunch?"

"It was OK, I guess. Mike wanted my opinion about whether he should arrest Mack Emory for murdering R. V."

I had expected some kind of reaction from her when I said that. Instead, she asked simply, "What'd you tell him?"

"I told him my gut feeling was that Mack wouldn't have murdered R. V. Beyond that, I couldn't help him."

"My intuition tells me the same thing," Jill responded. "Is Mike not going to arrest Mack because of your opinion?"

"I expect we'll hear about his arrest on the evening's news. Anything else going on?"

"Actually, yes. Robert called right after you left. He wanted to know if you'd like to ride with him in the morning to the farm. I told him you'd call him when you got back."

"Cool. I'd love to do that. I'll give him a call right now."

Chapter Twenty-One

Robert picked me up at seven the next morning, and we headed toward Hendry County. I knew that during the growing and harvesting season, he traveled to the farm almost daily. Some of the other guys in town had previously been asked to ride out there with him, but this was a first for me. I was actually honored to be asked to go with him. Robert, I knew, had semiretired from active farming, and his sons were actually responsible for most of the direct management of the operation. But Robert, from what I'd been told, still liked to keep an eye on things.

My experience with farming is limited. Granted, my ancestors in Florida were farmers, but that was at least a couple of generations in the past. While some of my family grew citrus and raised cattle, I personally had only touched agriculture enough when I was growing up to know that the farming lifestyle, at least at that time in my life, wasn't for me. I understood enough about it to know that I have a ton of respect for farmers, understanding clearly that it's not an easy way to make a living. I can still remember as a kid hearing my grandfathers worry about there being not enough rain—or, alternatively, sometimes stressing when the storms and hurricanes came about there being too much rain. I can remember well the many worried nights we spent huddled around thermometers in their groves, hoping against hope that clouds would drift in to keep the freezing temperatures from falling further into the grove-killing zone. And I remember clearly the great freezes of the 1980s that wiped out almost all the citrus in Central Florida. In effect, those few hours of bitter cold destroyed an entire way of life. Yes, I understood well that farming is not an easy way to make a living. I was looking forward to getting to see how Robert and his sons did it.

We headed off the island and took Florida State Road 78, more commonly called Pine Island Road, east. This road runs parallel to the Caloosahatchee River on its northern bank. Once we were past North Fort Myers, we jogged over to the south side of the river and turned east again, this time on State Road 80, the road to Labelle.

This town of fewer than five thousand inhabitants is the county seat of Hendry County. Its name comes from combining the names Laura and Belle, the two daughters of Francis A. Hendry, a pioneer cattleman who organized the town on the bank of the Caloosahatchee River in the 1800s. It began as a farming town, and it essentially remains one today. It is about as far removed from the glitz and glamour of Naples and the other coastal enclaves of wealth and fashion as it is possible to get in Florida. As we drove through the town, before turning north toward the farm, I thought that it looked like a friendly, comfortable sort of place. The thought crossed my mind that I might not like it as much if

I were one of the migrant farm workers trying to make a living in the surrounding fields. But I didn't dwell on that, preferring instead to pick Robert's brain about his farming activities.

"Robert, what do y'all grow this time of the year?" I asked.

"We grow melons in the winter and tomatoes in the spring. Right now, we're just finishing up melon season. We've still got about a quarter of our fields to pick and ship out. I'm anxious to get that done as soon as we can. Prices are strong now, since we've got the only melons in the whole country that are ready. In a couple of weeks, though, the fields all over the rest of Florida and South Georgia will be ready for harvest. When they come in, we won't be able to give away our stuff. We'll just have to plow them under and get ready for tomatoes."

"Wow!" I said. "I had no idea there was such a narrow window of time for you to get your melons to the market."

"Yeah, and it's not only time that matters. Another factor is the temperature around the rest of the country. If it's warm, everyone wants melons, and the price will be good. If it's cold? Not so much. Thankfully, it's sweltering in the Northeast right now. We can sell all we can pick."

About that time, we turned off the pavement onto a dirt road that was blocked by a locked gate.

"My property starts here," Robert said. "Do you know how to open and close a gate?"

"Oh, hell yeah," I said. "That's about the extent of my agricultural expertise, but that's one thing I excelled at as a kid."

I quickly walked to the gate and undid the chain that held it closed. I walked the gate open to let Robert drive his SUV through, then closed and locked the gate again.

As I climbed back in the cab of the Robert's big Lincoln, he said, "Thanks. It looks like you might have done that a time or two before."

"Yeah," I answered. "But I'm a little out of practice. I haven't done it for a very long time. Are these all your fields?"

I was looking at freshly plowed fields that stretched away almost as far as I could see. The loamy dirt looked rich and smelled fertile.

"These are my fields, but they're not all my fields," Robert said, laughing. "This is just one of my four farms. In addition, I lease several more. Now hang on. It might get a little rough on this road."

Robert was right. The road had its share of dips, swells, and potholes, but the big Lincoln did a fine job of isolating us from these imperfections. A few minutes later, we had navigated the perimeter of the first fields, driven around several large cypress heads, and followed the road into a new section of fields—this time unplowed fields with melons still growing in them. Robert stopped his truck alongside one of those fields. I could see a group of eight or ten men walking down rows, accompanied by a large field wagon being pulled by a tractor. As I looked more closely, I could see men bending over to cut the stems off the melons in the field. Then they would pick the fruit up and toss it to another man walking alongside the wagon. Those men would then toss the melons up to other men standing in the wagon, and they in turn would carefully stack the melons on a pile on board.

"Wow!" I exclaimed. "I bet those guys are tired at the end of the day."

"Nah, they're used to it. You know, that's what they do. I can still remember picking melons when I was a kid. A couple of days in the field cutting melons will toughen you up, all right."

"Are those guys your employees?"

"Not really. They're contracted. I tell the labor company when and how many I'll need, and they show up ready to work on the days specified. I've got contracts already signed for three years out."

"I had no idea. Are those guys Americans, or Mexicans, or what?"

"I have no idea," Robert answered. "Frankly, I don't want to know. That's what the labor company gets paid to worry about. Now, come on, and I'll show you the rest of the operation."

We drove for approximately another mile, passing both plowed and unplowed fields, before arriving at a large packing shed. It was a couple of hundred feet long and probably fifty feet wide. On one side, I could see field wagons backed under the shed, and on the other side were several large tractor-trailer rigs. In between, dozens of men were busily at work.

"What's going on here?" I asked.

"This is where the melons come in from the fields. We unload them, grade and inspect them, and pack them on the semis for transport to the ultimate buyers."

"So, if you don't mind my asking," I said, "who are the buyers?"

"Mostly large supermarket chains. That one truck on the end is an Arkansas truck, if you know what I mean. The one on this end is going to Lakeland. But we also sell to distributors who, in turn, sell to smaller outlets. I don't want to ever become overly reliant on any one buyer. If you do that, you can get put in a bind."

"I had no idea the magnitude of your operation. I'm impressed," I said.

"Oh, this ain't nothing," Robert said, casually dismissing my compliment. "This is just one farm. And you should have been here a couple of weeks ago, when we were really pumping the melons out. I love it then. Everybody's making money, and everybody's happy. The guys in the shed are singing, the guys in the field are singing, and you'd better believe I'm singing, too."

"I'd like to see that," I said. "Is this the same kind of operation that R. V. was running?"

As I said those words, I could see a cloud pass over Robert's face, and the happy grin that had been there when we were talking about melons was immediately replaced with a nearly expressionless glare. For a moment, he just stared out the front window of the truck and said nothing.

Finally, he spoke, "Yeah. R. V. ran an operation much like this, just maybe a little smaller. We grew up together, you know? I sure am going to miss that guy."

"I didn't know that, Robert. I'm sorry."

"That's all right. I just want to see whoever killed him get what's coming to him."

"Do you have any idea who that might have been?" I asked.

"We can talk more about that on the way home," Robert said. "Right now I've got to go and talk with my son. You can hang out here and watch this some more or, better yet, take the truck and drive down this road about a half mile to the north. You should be able to see all the wild turkeys and deer you'll ever want to see. Just be careful; you might find some bears out there, too. They love busted-up watermelons."

"Sounds like fun," I said. "When do you want me back?"

"Give me about an hour. That should be plenty of time for me to take care of business and hang out with the guys a bit. When you come back, we'll drive into town and get some lunch. There's a great barbeque place I'll take you to."

"You got it," I replied.

Chapter Twenty-Two

I drove in the direction Robert had suggested and parked at the edge of a large field. I turned off the engine, put the windows of the truck down, and watched. This field looked as if it had only recently been picked. There were still a few melons left on the vines, but most of those were either undersized or misshapen. I could also see the remnants of a fair number of busted melons lying on the ground, their juicy flesh souring in the morning sun.

Robert had been right about the wildlife. After my eyes adjusted to the glare, I could see several sizable flocks of turkeys grazing on the grass that bordered the field near a cypress head. I counted twenty-three birds, but there were certainly more keeping watch from the trees. I could also make out, farther toward the middle of the field, a large herd of deer. Twelve doe were contentedly dining on the grass that was growing around a small pond. The herd's buck, however, was eyeing me suspiciously.

I scanned the field repeatedly, hoping to catch sight of the bears Robert had cautioned me about, but it wasn't until just before I needed to return to meet Robert that I finally saw them. I watched in amazement as three animals meandered into the field from the far side of the cypress head. The one leading the group was significantly larger; I assumed this was the mama bear, trying to teach her two cubs about the joys of eating watermelons. The cubs, for their parts, seemed, like kids anywhere, to be having too much fun to be closely focused on the lesson. As I watched, with a grin spreading across my face, I could see the youngsters rolling across the furrows, leaping on top of each other, mischievously fighting, and just generally having a really good time. The mama bear, appearing to totally ignore the cubs' foolishness, found a satisfactory spot to dine. I watched as she selected an intact melon, laid it on the ground, and used her massive paw to open the fruit. She then picked up one half of the open melon and brought it up to her mouth. She didn't put the piece down again until there was nothing left except the clean green rind. Then she picked up the other half of the fruit and devoured it in the same fashion. Then, ambling along slowly in the way happy bears do, she found another appealing morsel, sat down, and began to eat again. The cubs, for their parts, were now taking turns drinking juice from the split melons, happily tossing the dripping rinds at each other, all the while rolling and tumbling like playful kids.

I could have watched this blissful family outing for hours, but I knew better than to keep Robert waiting. The last thing I wanted to do was make him late for lunch. Me, either, as far as that goes. As I started the truck and turned it around, I noticed that the noise and motion had disturbed the idyllic scene I had been enjoying. Now all the creatures were running in an alarmed fashion toward the protection of the nearby swamp. I hoped that they would come back after I was gone.

As I pulled up at the shed, I could see Robert standing with several of the guys who had been unloading one of the field wagons. Since they were all laughing, I deduced they must have been sharing jokes. As I got out of the truck to move to the passenger seat, I could see Robert put an arm around the shoulders of one of the workers, while moving his other arm in an animated manner, waving apparently to amplify the key points of the yarn that he was spinning. It must have been a good one, because as he finished, I could see everyone bending over laughing with their hands on their knees. Once he'd finished, Robert waved so long to the group, walked quickly to the truck, and climbed in.

"Robert," I said, "were you speaking to them in Spanish?"

"Yeah. I know just enough to be able to tell a dirty joke." He chuckled. "Did you see any wildlife?"

"Sure did. Bunch of turkeys and a good-size herd of deer. I even saw a mother bear and two cubs. They were having a great time eating leftover melons, but I would guess bears must be a real problem for your fields."

"Yeah, they can be. In fact, they're getting to be a real nuisance."

"So," I said, "how do you keep them out of your fields?"

"Well, about two weeks before the melons start to ripen, I hire a couple of guys to drive around the fields at night with some air horns and floodlights. Their job is to try to make enough racket to scare them away. Of course, in the old days, we'd have just shot them, but you can't do that anymore. Now, if they get to be a real problem, we'll call the FWC. We can request that they come trap them and get them out of here. You've got to pay attention to Yogi and his pals. If not, they can wipe out a whole field of melons pretty quickly."

"Yeah. I can see how that could be a problem. You said you've got a good barbeque place in mind?"

As I had hoped, Robert warmed quickly to this query. "Yeah. Arnold's. It's one of my favorites. It's in Labelle."

"So," I said half-jokingly, "I assume a guy named Arnold runs the place?"

"No." Robert laughed. "He used to, but not anymore. Old Arnold died about ten years ago. Now his son, Larry, is in charge."

"But it's still good?" I asked.

"Heck, in some ways it's better now than when Arnold was cooking. I think he'd got a mite set in his ways, if you know what I mean. Larry's kicked it up a couple of notches."

"So what's your favorite thing there to eat?" I asked.

"That's a hard question to answer, since it's all good. But, my go-to lunch item is the 'Labelle Special.'"

"What's that?" I asked.

"Basically, a pulled-pork sandwich stacked with coleslaw, grilled onions, cheese, and barbeque sauce. It's hard to beat."

"You've sold me," I said. "It sounds delicious."

Chapter Twenty-Three

Arnold's BBQ was located on the western edge of town, along-side State Highway 80, a road labeled within the city limits as Hickpoochee Avenue. I asked Robert what the name meant.

"That is what the Indians used to call this area," he said. "It means 'little prairie.' I guess the town's founders wanted something to remind them that all the land around here used to belong to the Indians. Back, that is," Robert said, laughing, "before the settlers slaughtered the Indians and took it from them. But who am I to judge? That land is how we make our living today—and a damn fine living it is!"

In the fashion of great BBQ joints everywhere, the restaurant was housed in a one-story wooden building that had obviously been expanded several times over the years. The front, and obviously original, part of the building was actually constructed of logs. The main entrance was still in that portion of the building. Behind this, and to the west, were more modern wooden additions. And, behind it all, a tall smoking chimney emitted drifting whiffs of oak woodsmoke that carried, even through the truck's rolled-up windows, smells that promised an excellent meal was to come.

Robert, surprisingly, found a just-vacated parking spot under the limbs of a large, spreading live oak at the far edge of the crowded parking lot. We both recognized how fortunate this find was. In many climates, diners covet spots nearest the front door, but not in Southwest Florida. Here, shade, at least at lunchtime, is more valued than distance. We exchanged knowing glances, exited the SUV, and walked toward the front door.

The sign over the front of the building was simple and to the point; it said "Arnold's" in bold red letters on a white background. Beneath that, in a smaller and more discreet black font, was the restaurant's slogan: "The Best BBQ in Town."

I reached the heavy wooden door first, opened it for Robert, and followed him inside.

Before he could say anything, I could hear the young, attractive hostess standing behind the greeting station welcome Robert.

"Good afternoon, Mr. Parrish. You want your usual table?"

"I most certainly do, Miss Mandy, but not before you give your old uncle a great big hug!" he replied.

"Oh, Mr. Parrish, you know I always do that." With that, she stepped out from behind the stand, leaned against Robert, and gave him a welcoming squeeze.

As soon as that small-town greeting was out of the way, she said, "Now, y'all just follow me."

Robert waved me ahead of him, and I began to gladly follow Mandy. While I was anxious to reach our table, it didn't take me long to understand that Robert had more pressing duties to perform. Specifically, it seemed like almost everyone at the tables we passed knew Robert and wanted to greet him. Many, in fact, wanted to engage him in conversation.

As I made my way toward the back of the dining room, I could overhear some of the dialogue. "How're your melons doing, Robert?" someone asked. Another queried, "Robert, how do you think the price of 'maters is going to be this year?" A female voice instructed, "Robert, you be sure and tell Miss Georgia hello, and y'all stop by the next time you're in town. I've got a jar of homemade guava jam that I'd like to give her." I was already well into perusing the lengthy, sauce-stained menu by the time Robert finally made it to the table.

"I'm sorry, Jim," he said. "Everyone always wants to talk."

"Not a problem, Robert," I answered. "I grew up in a small town, too. I know how it is. But, Robert," I said with a smile on my face, "I've got to ask you a question. Are you really Mandy's uncle?"

He grinned and said, "Well, of course I am. At least that's what I tell all the cute little girls in town. It makes them feel so much better about giving me a big old hug! Truthfully, I've known all these kids since before they even started school, and most of them have been calling me 'uncle' for as long as they can remember. Now, do you see anything in that menu that looks good?"

"I sure do," I answered. "I think I'm going to have your Labelle Special, an order of fried okra, a side of coleslaw, and some unsweet tea. How about you?"

"Pretty much the same, but I'm going for a side of fried green tomatoes and a big glass of sweet tea."

"Those wouldn't be your tomatoes, would they?" I asked.

"As a matter of fact, they are," Robert answered. "I don't grow any okra."

"Well, I'm changing my order to green tomatoes, too," I said.

"I like your way of thinking, Jim."

Our waitress, an older, matronly looking woman who addressed Robert as Bobby, efficiently and pleasantly took our orders, commenting on our request for fried green tomatoes.

"Bobby, those tomatoes of yours are flying off the shelf. Besides BBQ, that is our most popular item right now. I'll hate it when we can't get 'em anymore."

"Well, Aunt Fran, don't you worry about that. I've got some more just starting to come in now, and I've got more behind them. We should be able to eat them 'maters for at least another couple of months. How're your grandkids doing?"

"Oh, they're all fine. I don't know if you've heard, but Jimmy just joined the marines, and Emmy had another little girl."

"No, I hadn't heard that. How many kids does Emmy have now?" Robert asked.

"She's got three, two girls and a boy. She says this is going to be it."

"Well, three's a good number. How's Big Jim doing?"

"He's fine. He's driving for Walmart now, so he's home almost every night. Now that I'm getting older, that's a good thing," Fran answered.

"You be sure and tell him I said hello, Aunt Fran."

"I'll do it," she replied. "I'll have your food out in a minute."

After she'd gone, I said to Robert, "Labelle sure seems like a friendly kind of place."

"Yeah, for the most part. We pretty much all know one another. We don't see that many strangers, so normally we just do our best to get along."

Robert and I then turned to savoring the cooling briskness of our iced teas. There's nothing much better, at least for those of us raised in the South, than a cold glass of tea on a hot day. As a kid, I always drank sweet tea. And, that's still the preferred option for many. But, for the past forty years, or so, I've sworn off sugar, and now I always ask for my tea to be unsweetened. I'd just taken a long sip from my glass when I noticed the large ring on Robert's right ring finger. It looked to be crafted from solid gold, with initials prominently displayed on the top surface, and what looked like they could have been footballs raised on both sides. It looked to me like it could have been a college bowl ring, or maybe even a Super Bowl ring—it was that big. I had to ask Robert about it.

"Robert, I just noticed the ring on your right hand. That's a damn nice ring. Did you get that for playing football?"

He laughed. "Oh, hell no, Jim. I never played ball. I was always too busy loading melons. But, I was awarded this for serving as president of the Florida Watermelon Grower's Association. I almost never take it off."

"Well, it's a very nice ring," I replied.

As we continued to enjoy our teas, I began to look around the restaurant, while Robert stared at the screen on his iPhone. I'd just started to question Robert about the huge preserved alligator hide stretched on a board mounted over the kitchen's food counter when I did a double take. Robert noticed my reaction and turned his head to look at what I had seen. Then, taking it in, he turned toward me. We looked each other in the eyes. I raised my eyebrows.

"Is that lady waiting tables on the other end of the room who I think it is?" I asked. "Is that Lois Anne Emory?"

"Yeah." Robert chuckled. "I was wondering how long it'd take you to recognize her. She's been working here for about a week. This is her brother's place. Arnold, of course, was her dad. Mack must have cut up Lois Anne's credit cards and closed her bank account, so I guess she needs to make some money now."

"Can't blame him for doing that," I suggested.

"Nope. Not a bit," Robert agreed.

He had just begun to relate the history of the displayed alligator hide when we noticed a commotion at a booth Lois Anne had just begun to wait on. It was occupied by two young men; I guessed they were both in their late twenties. Each of them wore jeans and had dusty work boots on their feet. One was wearing a blue polo shirt, with the name of some business embroidered above the left chest. The other wore a long-sleeved chambray shirt, the tail of which was tucked tightly into his form-fitting jeans. The shirt's arms were neatly rolled above his biceps in what I took to be a conspicuous display of large, possibly steroid-enhanced, muscles.

As we watched, we could see the man in the chambray shirt start to paw at Lois Anne's backside. Then she swatted away his other hand, which had attempted to fondle one of her breasts. As soon as she'd deflect one grope, another would begin. Finally, in exasperation, she tried to slap her assailant across the face with her right hand, but her well-aimed swing was intercepted by the strong man's left hand. He smiled at her as he twisted her arm in a direction it wasn't meant to go. At this point, she began to scream and curse loudly.

Several men in the room, Robert included, had gotten up to intervene, but before they could reach the table, a heavily built man had emerged from the kitchen with a short aluminum baseball bat in his right hand. He quickly reached the rear of the booth where the struggle was taking place and, without a word, brought the bat down with force against the assailant's head. The loud *thonk* of the impact echoed around the hushed restaurant. The recipient of the blow instantly crumbled, his unfocused eyes still open as his limp body slid under the table and partially out of the booth. Its downward progress was not moderated in the least by the furniture encountered during its descent.

Lois Anne dashed for the kitchen as soon as the grip on her arm was released. The guy on the other side of the table was now sitting bolt upright, his arms raised in the universal signal of surrender, his eyes as wide as saucers.

The bat-wielding rescuer now pointed the bat at him and said, "John, if you know what's good for you, you'll get out of my restaurant, pronto. The cops are on the way, and if you're here when they arrive, I will have them arrest you for helping to assault my sister. Be sure to tell Jasper, when he wakes up, that I don't want to see either of you back in here again. And you tell him that if he ever, ever messes with my sister again, I won't use a bat next time. I'll use my sawed-off twelve-gauge. Now get out of here before I change my mind."

"But…" John began to whimper, "I…I rode with…"

With that, the large guy with the bat brought it upward, obviously ready and anxious to deliver another blow. That threat quickly caused John to reconsider his situation, and without another word, he ran toward the front door.

He hadn't even gotten past the hostess's stand when the man with the bat began to address the restaurant's diners. "Folks, I apologize for the commotion. Now, while we get this mess cleaned up, I hope you will go back to enjoying your lunch. When you finish, I want y'all to have some dessert, on the house."

As he turned to go, someone in the crowd began to clap, and soon the whole room was applauding. The large guy with the bat just waved it off, disappeared into the kitchen, and quickly returned with a busboy. Together they grabbed Jasper by the heels and dragged him out the back door. Jasper, I noticed, was still not awake as he was limply ejected from the building.

"Wow, Robert," I said. "I guess not everyone in Labelle is as friendly as I thought!"

He chuckled. "Sorry you had to see that, Jim, but at least we're going to get some free dessert."

"There is that," I said. "I take it that the guy with the bat was Larry?"

"Yep. And, as you can see, he really doesn't like anyone screwing around with his sister. Actually, he never has. For as long as I can remember, he's been dealing with guys who are stupid enough to mess with her. He just can't stand it."

"Obviously," I said. "Robert, I've got to ask, do you think he could be the guy who did in R. V.?"

"Nah. I wouldn't think so. They were good buddies—always fishing together and stuff like that."

"Did they go grouper fishing together?" I asked.

"Yeah, of course," said Robert. "But, come on, I think you may have been helping the sheriff's department too much."

"I don't know, Robert," I said. "Think about it. Larry and R. V. grouper fished together. Larry has a baseball bat and is not afraid to use it on anyone messing with Lois Anne. And, as we all know, R. V. was certainly 'messing' with her, if you know what I mean."

"Yeah, but Larry would never have killed R. V. Hell, they've been friends since they were kids. For God's sake, Jim, they even share a couple of Gator football season tickets! Trust me, if you start thinking Larry killed R. V., you'll be barking up the wrong tree again."

About that time, Aunt Fran brought our food to the table. Her mood was decidedly more subdued than before. She simply placed the plates in front of us, looked at Robert, sadly shook her head, and asked, "Y'all want some refills on those teas?" We both answered, "Please," and hungrily turned our attention to the meals.

I was not disappointed. The Labelle Special was everything Robert had promised, and the fried green tomatoes were probably the best I'd ever tasted. We contentedly finished our lunches, enjoying the meal in satisfied silence. Only when we'd finished the last remnants of our sandwiches did I ask Robert the question that had been bothering me since the day we'd found R. V.'s body.

"Robert, there's something I've been wanting to ask you. When we were at your party a couple of weeks ago, I noticed R. V. having an argument with some men by the pool. I didn't know the guys, but I remember thinking at the time that they must have been farmers like you. Do you have any idea who they were or what they might have been arguing about?"

"Yeah," Robert answered. "I saw them squabbling. One is a farmer from Arcadia. One is a rancher from outside of Lake Placid. And the other, the one probably taking R. V.'s side in the argument, is a real estate guy from the East Coast."

"So you do know what they were quarreling about?" I asked.

"Not sure," he said. "But it was probably the same thing R. V. had been carrying on about for a while."

"What was that?" I asked eagerly.

At that moment, I feared I had pushed my relationship with Robert too far. I could see him mentally wrestling with my question, apparently trying to decide whether to share what he knew. He sat back in the booth, stared out the window for a moment, and then took a long sip of his iced tea. Finally, it looked as if he had decided to confide in me. He leaned forward so he could whisper in a quiet, confidential manner.

"Jim, do you know what a 'conservation easement' is?" Robert asked.

"I think so," I answered. "Isn't that where the government pays a property owner not to develop land?"

"Exactly," Robert answered. "That's now a topic of great interest among many of the major landowners in Southwest Florida."

"Yeah. I've read something about that in the paper. But," I asked, "why were R. V. and those guys arguing about conservation easements? I thought most farmers were in favor of those deals."

"I think most of them are, but it's a little bit more complicated than that. I don't know that I want to be the guy who tells you."

"Robert," I exclaimed, "why wouldn't you want to tell me?"

"There's big money—and powerful people—involved in this," he said. "Trust me; you don't want to start stumbling around in the middle of what's going on. I know how you are. You won't rest until you get to the bottom of it, and I really don't want what might happen to you on my conscience."

"What about R. V.'s murder? You want the guy who killed him getting away with what he did? You want *that* on your con-science?" I asked.

"Jim, if there's one thing I've learned in my sixty years of liv-ing on this earth, it's that discretion is usually the better part of valor. And discretion usually starts with keeping your mouth shut. Unfortunately, that is something R. V. never learned."

"So," I said, "you do think that what R. V. was arguing about was what got him killed?"

"I don't know that," Robert said. "But it's possible."

"You said they were arguing about something to do with con-servation easements? Can you give me any more than that?"

Robert sat back in the booth, apparently thinking about whether he should respond, and if so, how. I watched him closely, thinking discretion was probably going to win out. For a while he stared down at his plate. I kept quiet, giving him time to process what was on his mind. After a lengthy pause, he leaned forward again and said quietly, "Does the name *Asa Parsons* mean anything to you?"

"I know there's a person by that name who's the commissioner of agriculture for the state of Florida. Is that who you're talking about?"

"Yes. Asa is not only the agricultural commissioner, but he is also planning to run for governor in two years. At this point, he's the odds-on favorite to be elected. He's kind of the Republican Party's fair-haired child. Good-looking, redheaded guy who reminds you a little bit of Opie from Mayberry. Today he likes to project an image of himself as being a squeaky-clean, country-boy politician. But, like anybody running for political office, especially the office he's now running for, he needs money—lots of money—to get elected. There are no secrets in any of this, but if you want to know more about what could have happened to R. V., the funding for Asa Parson's campaign would be a good place to start digging. Now, you want some free pie?"

Chapter Twenty-Four

We got back to Saint James City a little before six o'clock. I was dying to tell Jill what had happened during the day and what Robert had shared with me, but I'd forgotten that it was canasta night. She was heading out the door as I came in.

"Jill," I said, "you're not going to believe what happened today in Labelle. I think I might have two new leads on why R. V. was killed!"

"That's nice, honey," she said, as she brushed past me on her way down the outside stairs. I noticed she was using pot holders and holding a hot casserole dish. "I'm running late. We can talk about your theories when I get home. There are some leftovers in the fridge. Love you. Bye."

With that, she was gone, my balloon of excitement deflating as she drove away. The rapidly dispersing fragrance of the departing casserole only served to add to my disappointment. I could feel a sulk beginning to develop. My first inclination was to look in the refrigerator to see what I might find to nuke in the microwave for supper. But, truthfully, the Labelle Special was not even totally digested yet, and I knew more food was the last thing I needed. I considered plopping myself down in the recliner and watching the news on TV, but doing that was sure to depress me even further. So, instead, I decided it would be better if I were to do something constructive, something like seeing what I could learn about Asa Parsons.

I sat down in my recliner, but rather than flipping on the boob tube, I opened my iPad and Googled "Asa Parsons." As usual with a search of this nature, I discovered tons of information.

I started with the basic stuff to be found in a Wikipedia reference. I found that he was forty-two years old. He'd held his current office for six years, winning his latest reelection campaign comfortably with 60 percent of the vote. Prior to that, he had served his constituents as a US representative for five terms, and before that, he'd been a state representative for two terms. He'd been born in Polk County and, interestingly to me, had attended the same high school, albeit many decades later, that my father had graduated from. He had earned a bachelor of science in agricultural economics from the University of Florida. Doing the math, I could see that he'd probably never held a real job other than an elected office in his adult life. But nothing, I thought, was especially suspicious about any of that. In fact, at this point, I was already starting to despair of ever being able to find a link to anything in the least bit nefarious. But then I dug a little deeper.

One of the next articles established without a doubt that Parsons did, indeed, plan to run for governor in the next election. The incumbent had to leave office because of term-limit restrictions, and the Republican Party's powerbrokers had obviously anointed Asa as his heir apparent. Toward that end, the article noted that Parsons had already raised in excess of $5 million toward his campaign. That amount of money seemed surprisingly large. Robert, apparently, had been correct when he'd said Parsons needed money for his political ambitions. This article also included a listing of the top ten donors to the commissioner over the past year. I saw that the Association of Florida Business had provided almost a half million dollars; the Farmers Association had contributed more than $300,000; Florida's two largest electric utilities had provided similar amounts; the Fertilizer Council of Florida had anted up slightly less than a quarter million; the Sugar Coalition had provided that much as well; and the state's largest grocery chain had donated $150,000. As I scanned the list, the story was the same—all the donors were among the heaviest political hitters in the state. As I studied the list, I had to suspect that most, if not all, of the donors were regulated by the Florida Department of Agriculture, the very organization Parsons led! To me this arrangement seemed, at the least, odd. I thought, *Corruption in politics! Imagine that. Nothing that takes place in that cesspool ever surprises me.*

It wasn't until I rephrased the Google query that I found something I thought could have been possibly related to what Robert had hinted about.

"Ex-Congressman Got Millions in Questionable Land Deal!" was the headline on the *Orlando Sentinel* newspaper article.

Finally, I thought that I might be getting somewhere. Robert had indicated that R. V. and the others had been arguing about some kind of land deal. Could this be what he had meant? I read further with interest.

What I quickly learned was that Parsons (who at that time had been the third-highest-ranking Republican in the US House of Representatives) and his brother had become very rich men about a decade previously, when they had entered into an agreement to sell two thousand acres of land to an agency of the state of Florida: the South Florida Water Management District. In exchange, they'd received over $25 million. That was interesting, but it wasn't until I learned that this same land, a year before, had been valued at only $5.5 million that I found something suspicious. My suspicions were further piqued when I read that, at the time of the sale, the state agency that bought the land had said it only had a need for six hundred acres of the land it acquired at this inflated price. The rest, it had argued, was necessary to facilitate the acquisition of the land it really needed. At that, I almost gagged. As I read further, the article pointed out that now, after almost a decade, the state had actually used fewer than 150 acres of the acquired land. The Parsonses' cattle, as allowed in the agreement, were still grazing on the property.

As I had read this, it was clear that the deal smelled. As I read further, the sale began to positively stink—reeking of dishonesty, mismanagement, and fraud. I was beginning to suspect that honest Opie might have actually been a crook!

A year before the sale, the land had appraised at $5.5 million, and the district had offered to buy it at that price. The Parsons family, however, had been unwilling to sell. Later that year, at the urging of the Parsons family, the district agreed to seek another appraisal, and surprisingly, consulted with the Parsons family in the selection of the appraisers to be used. Eventually, two of the three appraisers hired had been suggested by the Parsons family.

Interestingly, I thought, one was a gentleman by the name of Tony Porter, a realtor who I noted lived in Palm Beach, on Florida's east coast. Not surprisingly, the new appraisal, conducted with the inclusion of the Parsons family's hand-selected appraisers, showed that the land's value had, for some reason, dramatically soared in the past year. A few months later, the district agreed to pay $25.5 million for the land, an amount that was significantly higher than even the appraisers' increased values. To add insult to injury, the family's attorney was awarded fees of almost $4 million, an amount over and above the negotiated price for the land. At the end of the day, the state ended up paying almost $30 million to acquire land that a year before had been valued at only a little over $5 million. Needless to say, this was a very, very sweet deal for all concerned—for all, that is, except the state's taxpayers.

The water district's inspector general, I learned, had repeatedly criticized this, and other land acquisitions, then being made by the district. He had noted that the appraisal process lacked essential controls and that the lack of these controls had resulted in a number of questionable appraisals. He had suggested that all appraisals should be competitively bid and that the independence of the district should be protected by ensuring that the appraisal process was kept separate from the acquisition process. He had also objected to allowing landowners to have input into the district's selection of appraisers. The article noted that all of these suggestions had been completely ignored during the Parsons negotiation. I noted at the end of the article, without a great deal of surprise, that this inspector general was no longer with the district.

Finally, I read a discussion that compared the per-acre price that the Parsons family had received for their property to the current value of similar land in the area. The commissioner's family had been paid over $12,500 per acre. Today, similar property in the area was valued at only $4,000 per acre. The article went on to note that there was not now, and never had been, any significant threat of commercial development in the area. The land was, and still is, basically swampy pasture land.

"Jeez," I said to myself. "I thought political corruption was bad when we lived in Alabama, but the scope and brazenness of that was really nothing compared to what's going on here."

I had actually read in the newspaper a few days before that one pundit had claimed that, in matters of political corruption, Florida was ranked second worst in the country. I had questioned that assertion then, but not any longer. Not after reading about the Parsonses' swindle.

If you can't trust a squeaky-clean, country-boy politician who comes from the same small town your own dad grew up in, who the heck can you trust?

Still, I asked myself, *what does any of this have to do more broadly with conservation easements in Southwest Florida?* That, I decided, was the subject I needed to research next.

"A conservation easement is a voluntary legal agreement between a landowner and a land trust of a government agency that permanently limits uses of the land in order to protect its conservation values"—this was the first definition of the term that I found with Google. That seemed simple enough. But as I surfed further, I learned that this subject was not quite as straightforward as it at first appeared.

The first of many issues I uncovered was an assertion that, since these conservation easements are nearly always celebrated as a public good, there is rarely any serious open, independent scrutiny of the specific terms of the easements or public review of the costs and benefits associated with the purchase of these easements. In addition, since these deals normally allow the acquiring agency to look good by being able to claim that yet another piece of property was saved from the evils of development, the agencies are usually anxious that the deals get done. Further, there is rarely anyone with direct responsibility to watchdog these deals for the public interest. Consequently, the whole process is frequently open to abuses in the appraisal process. I also learned that, all too often, agencies may enter into conservation easements for properties that would likely never have been developed anyway.

When I had finished reading these articles, I thought, *It sounds like the Parsonses' deal was a clear example of just these kinds of abuses.* I closed down the iPad, leaned back in the chair, and exhaled deeply. My conclusions were that, for sure, Asa Parsons was a shameless political crook who had enriched himself at the public trough. Secondly, the property-appraisal process in Florida was definitely open to abuse. And finally, conservation easements, while potentially being valuable tools, were, unless carefully scrutinized, open to significant misuse. *But what,* I wondered, *does any of this have to do with R. V. and the argument between the group of farmers that took place at Robert's house?*

Knowing the little I did about R. V.'s nature, I couldn't imagine him being opposed to potentially enriching himself by selling something at an overvalued price to the state. So did that mean he'd been trying to convince the others to go along with the crooked deal? And, if he'd been doing that, why would any of the powerful interests want to kill him? It just didn't make any sense.

By this time, my head was starting to ache. I decided it was time to forgo any further attempts at being constructive. Instead, I chose to treat myself to something from my Scotch whisky cabinet. I'd just put an ice cube in a glass and poured several fingers of a particularly fragrant whisky over it when Jill came in the door. I was so delighted to see her that I gave her a kiss before I'd even taken a sip from my drink.

"Jim," she asked suspiciously, "what have you been doing?"

"Nothing. I've just been surfing the web. Why?"

"I guess you don't quite seem like yourself." She laughed, pointing as she did at the bottle and untasted glass sitting on the counter. "Splurging, huh?"

"No…yeah…well, I guess. How were the girls?"

"Oh, they are fine. Let me go upstairs to change. You sit down and enjoy your drink. I'll be down to talk with you in a minute." She departed up the stairs to our bedroom on the third floor.

Chapter Twenty-Five

The enjoyment of single-malt scotch whisky is, I must confess, one of my many vices. Back in the days before retirement, back when I could actually afford to purchase a bottle of this top-shelf liquor, I had put together a modest single-malt collection. Actually, Jill might have mentioned a time or two that it was a little more than modest. And I was proud of it. I will admit, however, that the term *collection* might have actually been somewhat pretentious. My actual goal at that time had been to procure an example of every entry-level single-malt scotch available for sale in the United States. My goal had been to taste and compare them. And, eventually, over a number of years, I had achieved that. Like most drink collectors, I was always torn between the desire to possess and the desire to consume. In my case, of course, consumption won out. Consequently, the collection today is but a shadow of its former self, though it still contains enough wonderfully varied examples of the distillers' arts to allow me to occasionally enjoy a delightful taste of the Scots' famous water of life.

I was only a few sips into savoring the remarkable pungent, salty, smoky, seaweed-scented aromas of a cherished glass of Laphroaig when Jill returned. Truthfully, by that time I was already more into marveling, as I always do, about how different one whisky can taste from another than worrying about who might have killed R. V. Jill, however, was not so distracted. She clearly wanted to discuss the case.

"So, Jim, what did you learn today about who might have murdered R. V.?"

I proceeded to tell her, between enjoying additional sips of the wonderful whisky, what I'd seen happen at the BBQ place in Labelle. Then I shared what Robert had told me concerning a possible link between R. V.'s murder and Asa Parsons.

"That is interesting. You definitely need to call Mike Collins in the morning and tell him about this."

"Yeah. I guess so. I really don't want to start messing around in the middle of his investigation again."

"I know, honey," Jill said sweetly. "But you've got to let him know. This could be important. I've got to say, the link to Asa Parsons does sound kind of interesting. Don't you agree?"

"Yeah, I guess there could be a link, but I don't want to embarrass myself again. Mike's probably going to think that, this time for sure, I've gone off the deep end. You remember, don't you, that in past cases, I've pointed him toward the Collier family, the Royal Ranch, and most recently Big Sugar? And, I have to admit, none of these entities actually had anything to do with who committed the crimes. Now, if I tell him that Asa Parsons, the likely next governor of the state of Florida, has something to do with R. V.'s murder, he'll probably just start laughing. And, actually, I wouldn't blame him."

"I know. But, baby, still you've got to tell him," Jill insisted.

"All right. I'll give him a call. Now, how were the girls tonight?"

"Oh, we had a great time. We had wonderful oriental chicken and water chestnuts in lettuce wraps for dinner. They were delicious. We also had fried rice and spring rolls. And the sauvignon blanc was delightful."

"Delightful, huh?" I asked.

She grinned and said, "Especially delightful!"

"That's good. I'm glad y'all had a good time," I said. "Was Shirley Dodge with y'all?"

"Yeah. She came, and I think she had a good time. It has to be good for her to be able to get out and be around some people."

"How was she?" I asked. "Is she still having a hard time?"

"She actually seemed a lot better tonight. She only cried one time, but after that, you'd never know she was grieving at all, especially after her third glass of wine."

"Well, you did say that it was delightful!"

"Jim," she admonished me, "I'm trying to be serious here. It just made me wonder a little bit. You know, she kind of didn't really seem to be, I don't know, she just didn't strike me as really being all that sad anymore. I guess that just hit me as maybe just a little bit odd. But, then again, I've never been through anything like what she's going through, so I'm willing to give her the benefit of the doubt. Actually, I was glad that she was there. Now, how would you feel about going upstairs?"

"That wine must have really been good!" I commented.

"Delightful!" she said. "Why don't you pour yourself another drink and come upstairs to join me?"

Chapter Twenty-Six

The next morning, Mike Collins agreed to meet in Matlacha for lunch. Since the weather was especially pleasant, I suggested we eat at Island Seafood, a seafood market located on the bay just before you cross the bridge into the main part of the village. Not only is this locally owned business one of the best places in the area to buy fresh seafood (they own their own boats), but they will also cook you a great fish sandwich and let you eat it on an umbrella-covered picnic table by their dock. As far as I'm concerned, you really can't get more connected with the island way of life than by sitting on this dock, drinking a beer, eating a blackened grouper sandwich, and watching as a commercial fishing boat's catch is unloaded. I hoped Mike Collins would enjoy the experience as much as I always did. At the very least, I was sure he would appreciate the privacy provided by the table's relatively isolated dockside location.

I had arrived early to ensure possession of the best dockside table, and I waved at him as he drove into the shell-covered parking lot. As he exited his unmarked car and walked toward the dock, I had to admire how he'd been able to maintain his lean, athletic stature. I don't think he'd put on a single pound in all the years I'd known him. *Too bad*, I thought, *he couldn't say the same about me.*

"Good morning, Jim. Good to see you again."

"Morning, Mike," I replied in acknowledgment. "This table OK for you?"

He began to laugh. "Yeah. It's great! You couldn't possibly know this, but this spot and I have some history."

"History?"

"Yeah. When I was a kid, for a couple of summers, I actually crewed on a fishing boat that operated out of here. Trust me; that was a lot of fun. Lot of work, too. Back then there weren't any picnic tables to sit on, but I definitely remember drinking more than a few beers out here after we got through unloading the boats."

"Beer, huh? When you were a kid? Was that legal?"

"Come on, Jim. I haven't always been a cop, you know."

"I guess not. I've got to say, Mike, my admiration for you just went up a couple of notches. I had no idea that you'd ever worked on a fishing boat. That's pretty cool. It's pretty cool, too, that you used to break the law."

With that, Collins's demeanor became less cordial, and the twinkle in his eye disappeared. Instantly, he had become all business. "You said you might have something for me?"

"Mike, take it easy. I was just kidding with you. Why don't we go ahead and order, and we can talk while the food cooks. I'm going to have a grouper sandwich. They'll cook them grilled, blackened, or pan-fried."

"Damn, that sounds good, Jim. I'll have one, too. Make mine blackened."

Then, probably just because the 'devil made me do it,' I had to ask, "You want a beer with that?"

"Screw you, Story. Unsweet iced tea."

I left for the front of the building to place our orders, laughing to myself.

When I returned with two unsweet iced teas, I noticed Collins had gotten up from the table and was standing beside one of the commercial boats, having a conversation with a young crewman. After a couple of minutes, he returned to our table with the smile once again on his face.

"That was neat," he said. "That kid is actually a nephew of one of the guys I used to crew with. His uncle runs another boat, but he's at sea right now. The last time I saw his uncle was when we were sitting on this dock drinking beer way back when. Damn, those sure were good times. But, all right, Story, tell me what you've got."

"Mike, before I do that, you've got to promise me one thing."

"Maybe. What do I have to promise you?"

"You've got to promise me that you won't laugh at what I'm going to tell you, no matter how far-fetched it may seem."

With that the lieutenant began to chuckle. "Hell, Story. You know I can't do that! Your outlandish theories have always cracked me up." He took a deep breath and started to laugh again, before asking, "Who are you going to accuse this time—the governor?"

I stared into his eyes, not saying a thing.

Eventually, Collins picked up on my silence. As soon as he understood the significance of that, he stopped chuckling and said simply, "Not again!"

"Actually, I've got two stories for you, Mike. I was in Labelle yesterday with a friend of mine, a guy who farms over in Hendry County. He and R. V. were buddies. Anyway, after going to his farm, we had lunch at Arnold's BBQ. You know the place?"

"No. I've never spent much time out that way. What does BBQ have to do with who killed R. V.?"

"Probably not anything," I said. "But I think it's something you need to know. The restaurant where we ate is owned by Lois Anne Emory's brother, Larry. We saw him knock out a guy in the restaurant who was messing with Lois Anne. He whacked him on the back of his head with what looked like an aluminum shark bat and threatened to kill the guy if he ever messed with his sister again. Apparently, according to Robert, Larry has a history of dealing with guys who screw around with his sister. I thought that was something you'd probably want to hear about."

"Yeah, Jim, that is interesting. I'm glad you told me. But that doesn't sound like anything I'd laugh at you about. What else do you have?"

Fortunately, at this moment, the bell that announced our sandwiches were ready rang loudly, and I was able to postpone telling Collins my theory of how R. V.'s murder might be connected to Asa Parsons, likely future governor of the state of Florida. I went to the kitchen's window and brought the tray bearing our lunches back to the table. I used this interruption as an opportunity to change the subject and, as I distributed the food, asked Collins to tell me about his commercial-fishing experiences. As he told me the story, he seemed delighted to have an opportunity to relive that chapter from his youth. I gathered, from the way he laughed as he recounted these tales, that this had been a period of his life he had very much enjoyed. Then, after we'd finished eating, I further delayed the dreaded start of our conversation by volunteering to take our iced-tea cups inside to have them refilled. I made a point of walking slowly in both directions. When I finally returned, Collins forced the conversation, asking, "What was the second thing you wanted me to know?"

I took a deep breath, knowing that I couldn't delay any longer. I told him about my conversation with Robert and his suggestion that Asa Parsons might have some connection to the crime. I also told him about my research into the Parsons brothers' land deal and into the subject of conservation easements. Finally, I told him about the argument I'd observed at Robert's party.

Eventually, I stopped talking and focused on Collins. I was relieved to see he wasn't laughing. In fact, it appeared that he was actually thinking about what I'd just told him. Then, I noticed he'd shifted his gaze to the far northern reach of the bay. From the look on his face, I could sense it was his mind, rather than his eyes, that was focused on something, so I kept my mouth shut and just let him think. Finally, after a couple of minutes, his attention returned to the present, and to me.

"Jim, I appreciate you sharing both of these things with me. You were right to do this. This does indeed give me something else to look into."

"OK, Mike. I'm just trying to help, and I really don't want to get in your way."

"Yeah, I know that, and I do appreciate it."

"But I've still got to ask. Why haven't you arrested Mack Emory?"

I could see him sigh. "Hell, Jim! I probably should have, but he's not going anywhere. We've got his passport, and he knows better than to run. Bottom line, despite what the evidence shows, I'm still not convinced that he's the guy. What are your thoughts about that now?"

"Truthfully, I don't really know. But I'll tell you, in the back of my mind, there's something out there that's staring us in the face; there's something out there that we ought to be able to see. For the life of me, I don't know what it is. Sorry."

"Yeah. It's always like that, isn't it? If it comes to you, let me know. Hell, if it comes to you, call me, anytime, day or night. I don't care. Let's just get this mess over, and then we'll come back out here and drink some beer."

He got up to return to his car. I could see him smiling as he walked away.

Chapter Twenty-Seven

The rest of the week passed quietly. Toward the end of the week, Kenny and I went fishing on the northern end of the sound, up near Bokeelia. We first stopped off at the shoals that line the southern edge of Foster's Bay to catch white bait. One throw of my ten-foot-long bait net was all it took. Truthfully, the bait was so thick in the water that I was glad I caught only a few hundred fish. A friend of mine had told me earlier in the week that recently, with one cast, he'd netted so much white bait that he'd had to release the net's braille lines to let some of the bait escape before he'd been able to lift the net into the boat. We didn't have that problem.

White bait is what we call the small fish that, during the year's warmer months, invade the sound by the zillions. More formally, the bait is called "scaled sardine." In our waters, these fish are typically two to three inches in length. Most frequently they can be found on very shallow grass flats along the edges of the sound's shoals. If you're lucky, you will be able to see the bait in these areas, as they school together in aggregations of thousands of fish, sometimes causing so much of a disturbance that it looks and sounds like the drops of a heavy rainstorm falling on the top of the water. Today the fish weren't quite that thick, but still we had no trouble locating them. We eased onto the flat, shut the motor off, and drifted quietly into the middle of a sizable school of fish. Two minutes later, we were on our way.

As I put the boat on a plane to continue north, I thought, *You have to love it when a plan comes together.* I just hoped the day's fishing would be as successful.

As it turned out, we had a pretty good day. We each had our limits of trout in the box by noon, with Kenny proud to claim the day's largest fish. His measured a little over twenty-three inches nose to tail. Once we'd limited out on trout, we decided to try our hands at catching redfish. A friend of Kenny's had told him he'd recently seen several large schools of reds working the shallow waters of the shoals off the northern tip of Bokeelia. As it turned out, we saw them, too, but we couldn't catch them. We tried everything. We free-lined bait. We floated it under a popping cork. We even tried chumming with live bait. The fish simply didn't seem to be interested in what we were offering, but they were certainly there. It was frustrating, for sure.

We could see them serenely gliding by on the bar with the tips of their bronze-colored tails sticking out of the water. Then, periodically, there would be a literal explosion in the water as an unseen school of reds would attack an unsuspecting school of passing bait. There were fish on that shoal, all right, but none of them wanted to come home with us that day. Some days are just like that. We reminded each other that that's why it's called *fishing* and not *catching*. Eventually, we called it a day. Kenny and I concluded on the boat ride home that we'd sure like to go back up there sometime and try them again, but next time, we'd bring along some freshly cut mullet chunks to use as bait.

An hour later, the boat was on the lift. Kenny volunteered to clean the fish, while I transported the gear back into the house and washed down the boat. Twenty minutes later, Kenny left for home with a nice bag of trout fillets, and I went upstairs to talk with Jill.

"Hey, babe!" I said enthusiastically, as I entered the room. "We had a really good day. We caught—" I stopped talking as soon as I saw her sitting on the couch, the phone at her ear, her arm waving at me to shut up so she could hear what the person on the other end was saying.

I waited patiently, listening to her side of the conversation, and overhearing her say, "Are you sure?" A little bit later, she said, "And you're sure it was a man?" Sensing that some juicy gossip was probably being shared, I began to become more interested in the conversation.

"Come on, Georgia, you can't really believe that!" Jill argued. She listened for a few moments longer, then interjected, "But even if someone *did* sleep with her, that doesn't mean it was him." Again, she listened, before adding, "Well, that is interesting. But, still, you don't really know who it was, right?"

I walked around to the front of the couch, caught Jill's eye, and pantomimed with an exaggerated facial expression, and a display of upturned palms, the question "What?" Clearly, since she'd waved her arms at me in an obviously irritated fashion to indicate that I should go away, she wasn't ready to let me in on

THE FLORIDA RIG MURDER

what the conversation was about. Reluctantly, I went to the bathroom to clean up.

There are few things in the world more pleasant than taking a shower after a long day of fishing. It simply feels wonderful to cleanse your body of the salt spray, fish slime, suntan oil, sweat, and whatever else has managed to accumulate on your skin. Warm water, shampoo, and the suds from a good bar of bath soap will do wonders to rejuvenate you. This is an experience not to be hurried. And I didn't. In fact, I took so much time enjoying the pleasures of the cleansing that, by the time I had finished, I had forgotten about Jill's conversation. Clearly she hadn't. I walked back into the living room, feeling like a new man, and looking, I hoped, resplendent in clean canvas shorts and a fresh, crisp cotton fishing shirt. I suppose that, in the back of my mind, I was wishing Jill would be so taken with my transformation that desire might overcome her, leaving her unable to resist my planned suggestion that we could engage in a little afternoon delight. Of course, I should have known better. That kind of stuff only happens in the movies.

"Babe," she said as I walked in. "You're not going to believe what Georgia told me!"

Sensing that my ill-conceived plan was already coming apart at the seams, I answered with perhaps a little less enthusiasm than she had been expecting.

"Jim, damn it! Get over here, sit down, and listen. I think you'll want to hear what she told me."

I took a seat in the recliner facing her, feeling a little like an admonished schoolchild. "Yes, ma'am," I answered with what might have been a slightly exaggerated emphasis on the last word.

She glared at me to let me know she thought I was acting like an insolent adolescent. I got the message, understanding clearly that it would be in my best interest to start paying attention.

"Sorry," I said. "What *did* Georgia tell you?"

"You know Rachel, don't you? The lady who lives on the next block over."

"Yeah. Isn't she the woman who sometimes pet-sits? Don't we sometimes meet her on the street walking dogs?"

"Yes. That's right. I don't know if you know, but she also cleans houses for some folks."

"Yeah. I think I did know that. Doesn't she do Georgia's house?"

"That's right," Jill answered. "She cleans for Georgia once a week, and she was there working this morning. Well, Rachel also cleans for Shirley Dodge three days a week. Anyway, Georgia said that when Rachel came in this morning to clean, she seemed upset. So, you know how Georgia is. She just went right out and asked Rachel if something was bothering her. Georgia said that she figured Rachel must have had a fight with her husband or something, but she certainly didn't expect what Rachel finally told her."

"What'd she say? Is something wrong with Rachel?" I asked.

"No! Not with Rachel," Jill responded.

"So what was she so upset about?"

"Well, according to Georgia, it was because of what Rachel saw when she was cleaning Shirley Dodge's house yesterday."

Now, Jill had my total interest. "What in the world did she see that had her so upset?"

"Let me back up a bit. You probably don't know this, but according to Georgia, Rachel is very religious. Her faith, apparently, is very important to her."

"Didn't know that," I said, shrugging impatiently, hoping to convey silently that she should get on to the good part of the story.

"Hold on, Jim," Jill responded calmly. "Stay with me on this. It gets better. You, of course, know that R. V. Dodge has been dead for only a couple of weeks. Well, Rachel, being perhaps a little bit old-fashioned, was of the opinion that a woman who had just lost her husband, a husband whom supposedly she had loved for many years, should likely let more than just a few days pass before she started to entertain, shall we say, another man. Rachel, at first, said she wanted to get Georgia's opinion on whether she should continue to work for Shirley, given what she knew."

"Whoa! That is interesting," I exclaimed. "But how'd Rachel know that Shirley had been sleeping with another man?"

"Come on, Jim. Think about it. Maids get to see stuff that nobody else does. Stained sheets, for example. What's in the garbage. What's in the laundry. Things like that. Apparently, Rachel started noticing things right after R. V. was killed that didn't seem quite proper. At first, she thought it was just stuff that hadn't been cleaned up after R. V. had died. But, as time passed, and as certain evidence reappeared after Rachel had already cleaned it up, she was forced to conclude that Shirley had indeed been seeking solace from a gentleman acquaintance."

"Does Rachel know who the man is?" I asked.

"Well, that's the thing. I think she's worried it might be Robert."

"Robert!" I exclaimed. "Why in the world would she think that?"

"Because, yesterday, when she was dusting, she noticed a man's gold signet ring in a jewelry tray on the top of the dresser in

Shirley's bedroom. She noticed it because she'd never seen it there before. At first she thought it probably was just a keepsake of R. V.'s that Shirley had pulled out to remember him by. But when she saw what was on the face of the ring, she had to change her mind. There were three initials. In the middle was a larger capital *P*, and on each side of that were the smaller letters *R* and *A*."

"R. A. P.? Doesn't sound much like it was R. V. Dodge's ring, does it? Those initials mean anything to you?"

"Well, *R* could stand for Robert," Jill answered. "And Robert's last name *is* Parrish. The idea that this ring might have belonged to Robert apparently occurred to Rachel. Georgia said she thinks this was really the reason Rachel had wanted to talk with her. Rachel told Georgia she knew Robert had a ring like the one she saw at Shirley's house. Apparently, she remembered having seen him wearing it. Of course, that was the real reason Rachel wanted to make sure Georgia knew what was going on."

"Oh, come on! Not Robert. Not with Shirley Dodge. There's no way I would believe that," I exclaimed.

"Well, that's what Georgia believes, too. But, still, she's a little worried."

"Yeah, if I were her, I probably would be, too," I acknowledged. "Does Robert's middle name start with an *A*?"

"Adam," Jill said calmly.

"And you said he's got a signet ring with those same initials?"

"Yeah. Actually, it was a ring the Florida Watermelon Growers Association gave him in recognition of having served as that group's president. According to Georgia, it's been a tradition to present rings like that to all outgoing presidents. They've been doing it for fifty years or more."

"Yeah, I saw that ring on his hand when we were in Labelle. I wonder if there have been any other presidents of that group with those initials."

"I was wondering the same thing, and I asked her about that. But, Georgia said she only knew for sure about Asa Parsons. His first name is Randall. But there could have been others, too. She's planning to do some research on that."

"Was Robert's ring still in Georgia's house?" I asked.

"No. But Georgia said that wasn't unusual, because he wears it all the time. She said he hardly ever takes it off. Just to make sure, though, she asked Rachel to go back to Shirley's and hide the ring she'd found there. She asked her to hide it where no one could easily find it, but somewhere that it could have possibly fallen by accident."

"Wow! I sure hope Robert has that ring on when he comes home."

"He'd better!" Jill agreed.

Chapter Twenty-Eight

The next morning, a little after eleven, I was outside washing down the boat. I had recently started to use a new product called Salt Away. It's a highly concentrated but environmentally friendly detergent that does an amazing job on ridding a boat, and the insides of a boat's engine, of salt residue. I had quickly learned to love it. I had finished flushing the outboard and was beginning to wash down the deck and hull when Jill came out of the house and walked to the dock.

"Hey, babe," I greeted her, glad for the interruption.

"Honey, I'm going to lunch with Georgia and Roxie. We've got some stuff we need to talk about. There're plenty of things in the fridge for lunch. I won't be too long. We're not going off-island. See you in a bit."

"OK," I replied. "Y'all have a good time."

As she walked away, I regretted that I hadn't asked her if Robert had been wearing his signet ring when he'd come home last night. I reasoned that he probably had been. Otherwise, I doubted the girls would have been going out to lunch. Given that, I deduced that the girls were probably getting together to ana-lyze the story Georgia had shared last night. Roxie is a real estate broker in town and one of the card girls, and they are all thick as thieves. As I returned to washing down the boat, I laughed to myself, thinking that the three of them would probably be schem-ing to put together a plan, or more likely a trap, to establish who was actually sleeping with Shirley Dodge.

I diligently scrubbed the boat, using my boat brush and a bucket of suds, for almost an hour. The boat was positively shin-ing by the time I had finished. After that, I took some time to polish away the rust stains that had started to run from the deck hardware. When that was done, I went inside for lunch.

I had just finished my simple turkey and cheese sandwich when the phone rang. Seeing that it was an island number, I answered it.

"Jim, thank God you are there. This is Carolyn. Is Jill with you?"

Carolyn is another of the Card Girls. Jill and I had actually bought our house from Carolyn and her husband, Delmar. She is a part-time real estate agent in town, working out of Roxie's agency.

"No, Carolyn. Jill's not here. She went to lunch with Georgia and Roxie. What's wrong?"

"Well, hopefully nothing. But Nick and I are a little worried."

"Nick from the real estate office?"

"Yeah. You wouldn't know this, but Roxie always carries a SPOT, you know a personal-locating beacon, in her purse. After what happened to those female realtors on the East Coast last year, we all do that now. We want to make sure someone always knows where we are when we go out on a call with a client. You can't be too careful these days."

"Yeah," I said. "A SPOT is like a mini EPIRB, isn't it?" I asked. "Doesn't it use a GPS signal to track you?"

"Exactly. And if you have the device's tracking feature turned on, it will periodically send a signal marking your location to whomever you've authorized to receive it. Like I said, we all do that now. We've got them set to send out our locations every ten minutes whenever we go out with a client on a call. And we've got them programmed to send the signals to Nick's iPad. That way someone will always know where we are—just in case some weirdo is interested in more than just buying a house."

"Sounds like a good idea. But what's that got to do with Jill and the girls having lunch?" I asked.

"When was the last time you spoke to Jill?"

"When she left to meet Roxie and Georgia for lunch. I guess that was a little after eleven. You're starting to worry me, Carolyn. What's going on?"

"Nick just called me. He said he was getting a signal from Roxie's SPOT. It indicated that she was on a boat heading west out of Redfish Pass. He said that looked funny to him, because he knew Roxie had a showing today at two. So he tried to call her. When he couldn't get an answer, he called to ask me if I thought Roxie was going fishing today."

"She wasn't, was she? I mean, she and Georgia and Jill were having lunch together, right?" I asked.

Carolyn didn't respond.

"Carolyn?" I asked. "They were going to lunch, right?"

"Well, Jim, *not exactly*. They wanted me to go with them, but I couldn't, because I'm having a new sofa delivered in a few minutes."

"Carolyn, what do you mean by *not exactly*? If they weren't meeting for lunch, what *were* they meeting for?"

"Well, I promised not to tell anybody, but…"

"Carolyn, this could be serious. What were they up to?"

"Well, they were just breaking into Shirley Dodge's house today at noon!"

"Just breaking into Shirley Dodge's house! What in the hell were they thinking?" I shouted.

"Well, they weren't *actually* going to break in. Rachel was scheduled to clean Shirley's house this morning, and she promised to leave the front door unlocked when she left for lunch. Georgia wanted to have a look around to see if she could find any evidence about who had actually been there. She asked us all to go with her to help. It sounded like fun."

"But how did y'all know Shirley wouldn't be there?"

"Rachel told Georgia that Shirley had a doctor's appointment today in Cape Coral. They figured that, since she wouldn't be there, they would be able to get in and out without anyone ever knowing. And, besides, they thought that if they got surprised, they could always claim they were worried about Shirley and had just come by the house to check on her."

"But now we think Roxie is heading out into the gulf!" I exclaimed.

"And maybe not just Roxie!" Carolyn said.

"What's that supposed to mean?" I asked

"Well, I just called Georgia's phone, but I couldn't get an answer. I tried Jill's, too. Same result."

"So, Georgia and Jill could be on a boat with Roxie heading out into the gulf? Could they be on Roxie's boat?"

"Jim, you know Roxie doesn't have a boat," Carolyn reminded me. "If she were to ever go out in the gulf, she'd probably go out with Walking John on his boat. But I know he's up north right now. Hold on, Jim. I'm getting a new text message from Nick."

There was a pause before Carolyn told me, "Nick wrote, 'Still heading west—fast.' Then she asked, "Jim, what do you think is going on?"

"It sounds to me like somebody has gotten them. Have you talked with Robert yet?"

"Yeah. He's down at Woody's having lunch. I checked with him to see if Georgia was with him, but of course, I couldn't tell him what was really going on."

"Well, he damn sure needs to know now. I'm going to Woody's."

Chapter Twenty-Nine

Before I left the house, I called Mike Collins. Fortunately, he answered.

"Mike, I've got a problem—a big problem—and I need your help."

"What's up?"

"Jill and two of her friends have been kidnapped. They're being taken out into the gulf right now, probably to be disposed of. Hopefully, they're still alive."

"What the hell are you talking about, Story? Who's got them? Is it the governor? Or the commissioner of agriculture?"

"Mike, damn it, this is serious. I'm not making this crap up. Jill's in trouble, and I need your help—*now*!"

"OK, Jim, settle down. Now tell me what's going on, calmly."

"I don't have time to tell you everything, you're just going to have to trust me on this, but bottom line, Jill and a couple of her friends had gone into Shirley Dodge's house to look for evidence to establish who was having an affair with Shirley. I know that sounds bad, but I think the girls were just doing it on a lark. That doesn't really matter. All that matters right now is that I think they were discovered and captured by someone while they were there. And now they're all being taken out into the gulf, probably to be dumped. We know because one of the ladies, Roxie, who is a real estate agent, carries a SPOT beacon in her purse. Her partner at the office says it shows that, as we speak, they're heading due west out of Redfish Pass."

"They were breaking into a house?"

"Mike, we'll have to deal with that later."

"OK, Jim," Collins said sarcastically, "let's assume for a moment that somehow we can get beyond that little indiscretion. Maybe the girls are just going fishing. Or maybe they're just going for a joyride."

"Look Mike, I believe with a high degree of certainty, that they aren't doing that. Right now Jill and her friends are in a lot of trouble, and I need your help. I need your chopper to go after them."

"Can't do that, Jim. The gulf's out of my jurisdiction."

"Screw that, Collins. Call the coasties. Call the navy. Hell, call the president. I don't care who you call; I just need you to get off your skinny butt and go find Jill before something bad happens to her…if it hasn't already. Mike, you've just got to trust me on this. I know that I may have occasionally misled you in the past, but not this time. This is the real deal. I need your help!"

"All right. All right. I'll try to do something. Now, who's getting the SPOT's signals?"

"Fellow named Nick, down at the real estate office here in town."

"All right. I'll have one of my guys there in a couple of minutes. I'll call the coast guard and see if they can get a chopper up and a cutter under way, too. They'll be a lot quicker than we can be, but I'll have our boys scramble our bird, and we'll also get a boat on the water. Now, what are we looking for?"

"I don't know, Mike. But my best guess is that they're probably in R. V. Dodge's boat. It's a big, blue, center console, with three outboards. It's usually on the lift behind the Dodge's house. If they were kidnapped in that house, and if they're now on a boat heading into the gulf, I think it's logical that that's probably how they got there."

"That's all you've got?"

"Well, there should be at least one guy aboard, and three, maybe four, ladies. Mike, thanks. I really appreciate your help. But, look, we're going to be heading that way, too. Y'all better get to them before we do!" I hung up and called Kenny.

"Kenny, I'll pick you up at your street in ten minutes. We're going out into the gulf. Bring your gun."

I hung up before he could ask any questions, ran down the stairs to my car, and squealed out of the driveway, heading to Woody's six blocks away.

I slid the car under the Tiki Hut roof that adorns the front of the restaurant, the one with "No Parking" signs posted on each supporting pole. Before the dust from the tires had even begun to rise, I sprinted inside looking for Robert. He wasn't hard to find. He was sitting on a stool about halfway down the bar, looking relaxed and happy, a nearly empty tall glass of beer in front of him, and a half-eaten cheeseburger in his right hand, suspended between his mouth and the plate. On the bar in front of him was a platter, on which a half-eaten order of fries swam in a pool of ketchup. Robert had clearly been enjoying his lunch. I put an end to that.

"Hey, Jim, how're you—" he began as he saw me coming in the door. He didn't get to finish the greeting.

"Shut up, Robert! I need to ask you one question, and if you try to lie to me, I'll shove that damn burger so far down your throat you'll never eat again. Now, Robert, yes or no, have you been screwing Shirley Dodge?"

I looked at his face closely as he processed my out-of-the-blue question. As I scrutinized him, all I could see was confusion. I could detect no indication that he was trying to construct a deception. He carefully placed the burger on the platter, pushed it away, turned to face me, and looked straight into my eyes. His body was relaxed, showing no sign of preparing for either fight or flight. Then, he calmly, and simply, answered, "No."

At that point I looked away. As I did, I noticed his right hand resting on the bar. On the ring finger was a large, old-fashioned, gold signet ring. The initials RPA prominently displayed on its face. At that point, I had all the confirmation of innocence that I needed.

"Robert, do you know where Georgia is?"

"Isn't she with Jill? I thought they were going to lunch together."

"I think they are together, but they're in trouble. Has your big boat got fuel in it?"

"Full," he answered.

"Good. I'm going to pick up Kenny. We'll meet you at your house as soon as you can get there. Get some guns, and load them. We've got to go out in the gulf and find the girls. Somebody's got them."

With that I stepped away from the bar and ran toward the door. I glanced back as I went through it and saw Robert throw some bills on the bar and slide off his stool. I noticed the bartender watching with a shocked, confused, and openmouthed expression.

I spun the car's wheels leaving Woody's gravel parking lot and slid to a stop in front of Kenny's house no more than forty-five seconds later. He was standing beside the street, looking impatient, serious, and worried. I noticed that he had strapped a pistol belt around his waist and that a full holster was hanging heavily from that. He climbed into the car.

As I accelerated away, he asked, "What's up?"

"We're going out in the gulf to get Jill. I think she, Roxy, and Georgia have been kidnapped by whoever killed R. V."

"How are we getting there?"

"Robert's boat."

"That ought to get us there, and it ought to get us there quickly, too."

"Kenny, I just hope we can get there before it's too late. Mike Collins says he's sending the coast guard and some deputies, too."

I squealed around the few corners that separate Robert's house from Kenny's. As we pulled into his circular driveway in front of the waterfront mansion, I was disappointed not to see Robert's big Lincoln. Then I heard the sound of his SUV's tires protesting as they negotiated the same corners that we had just slid through. He squealed to a stop, hopped out, and began to move faster than I had ever seen him.

He yelled at us as he bounded up the stairs. "I'm going after the guns. Y'all get the boat off the lift."

By the time the thirty-four-foot-long center console was float-ing, Robert had joined us at the dock. He'd brought two twelve-gauge automatics, a powerful-looking hunting rifle with a scope, and a couple of bags of ammunition. I was impressed at the amount of firepower he'd had available at a moment's notice. He threw me the keys to his boat and began to hand the weapons to Kenny, who was already on board. Then, he said, "Jim, you drive. You're faster than me."

He didn't have to ask twice. By the time he was aboard, I already had the boat's big Mercury outboards fired up. Seconds later, I backed the boat away from the dock and spun it around to head out the bayou. Since the tide was high enough to allow it, I pointed the boat's bow toward the shortcut that leads through the slow speed manatee zone directly to the bay; there would be no wasting time today to dodge any basking sea cows. Normally, I care as much about protecting these lovable creatures as anyone…but not today—not when my baby was in danger.

A large center console moving at fifty knots per hour throws up a hell of a wake, especially in a no-wake zone. *Screw that,* I thought. *We aren't slowing down for anyone or anything.* Eight min-utes later, we were racing through the channel that leads to Redfish Pass. We didn't pay attention to the slow speed warning signs there, either. A minute later, we were in the gulf, our head-ing 270 degrees: due west.

At that point, I turned the helm over to Robert and called Mike Collins on my cell.

"Mike, we've just left Redfish Pass. We're heading due west at fifty knots. We'll be out of cell-phone range in a couple of minutes, but you can reach us on the radio with the handle "Big Melons." Now, what's happening?"

"The SPOT is still sending signals, and the boat's still heading west. They're out almost forty miles now. Coast guard has scrambled a chopper out of Saint Pete, and one of their cutters is coming out of Fort Myers Beach. Where do you think the boat's going?"

"My guess, and it's only a guess, would be that they plan to drop the girls near the same location where we found R. V.'s body. Fifty miles out—due west. That's where the chopper ought to go. That's where we're heading."

"Sounds reasonable to me, Jim. I'll let the coasties know. Are y'all armed?"

"Yep."

"Be careful, and let me know if anything goes down."

"You do the same."

We hung up. A few minutes later, we lost sight of land.

Chapter Thirty

The southeastern gulf is an empty place. No commercial traffic passes this way, and there's precious little in the way of recreational fishing this far offshore. The few boats that venture out here disperse over thousands of square miles of sea. There are no airplanes passing overhead. Hell, truthfully, there aren't even that many birds out here. It can be a lonely place.

As we sped west, all I could think of was how unlikely it would be that we would be able to find the girls if they were in the water. And that was assuming that they were still alive! From the deck of a bouncing boat, you can only effectively see for a few hundred yards. And that is in the daylight. I knew the sun would be going down in a few hours; in the dark, there would be no way we would be able to see anything, even with the spotlight on Robert's boat. We might be able to hear them if they yelled at us—sound does carry well over water—but we'd have to shut the engines off to hear anything. If we did that, we couldn't look for them. A shiver ran down my back, but it wasn't because I was cold. Rather, I'd just remembered that these waters were home to some of the largest, most fearsome man-eating sharks in the world. Hammerheads out here can grow to over fifteen feet in length. Makos can reach twelve. Hell, there are even great whites out here, too. Then, just as I was beginning to despair, I heard Mike Collins hail us on the radio.

As soon as we got on a working channel, Mike told us the tracking signal from the SPOT showed that the boat had come to a stop almost exactly where I had suggested it might. But then the SPOT, instead of continuing to send a tracking signal, had begun to transmit an SOS signal. Clearly, something bad was going down, but at least whoever was operating the SPOT was still alive. He said the coast guard's chopper was locked in on that location but it wouldn't be there for ten minutes. That wasn't good. A lot can happen in ten minutes, and we were still twenty-five or thirty minutes away. That cold chill returned to my spine. I thanked Mike for the information and asked him to let us know if anything changed— which is what he did a couple of minutes later.

"Jim, the boat is heading back in. It's coming right toward you now. Y'all get ready. You'll probably be able to see them soon."

Robert and Kenny had been listening to the conversation. We all looked at one another and slowly nodded our heads. Kenny quietly laid a loaded shotgun on the shelf that ran in front of the steering wheel. He handed me a similar weapon.

I took a long look at it, making sure I knew how it worked. Then I picked it up, and silently clicked the safety off and on, just to make sure I knew how to do it. It had been a long time since I'd fired a twelve-gauge, but I remembered that it would kick like hell. And I knew that it would make a heck of a lot of noise. As awful as it would be on the firing end of that thing, though, I knew it would be a heck of lot worse to be on the receiving end. I nervously fingered the safety one more time and thought that those guys coming toward us had made a big mistake when they had decided to hurt Jill. I looked at Robert. I could tell from the look on his face that he was thinking the same thing about Georgia.

I glanced back at Kenny. As I watched, he gazed through the scope on the rifle he was holding against his shoulder. I thought for a moment that he was going to fire the thing, but I had to chuckle after I realized he was only using the magnification to scan a passing squadron of pelicans. I noticed then that the Winchester he was holding had a magazine inserted in it—full, I hoped, of 30/30 cartridges. It was a serious weapon, one I suspected had brought down a lot of deer over the years. I also noticed that Kenny still had the pistol strapped to his waist. While I don't know that much about guns, I guessed, from having watched too many cop shows on television, that it was probably a Smith & Wesson .357 Magnum revolver. But, whatever it actually was, Kenny was definitely armed for combat, both long-range and short-range.

"Kenny," I said, "come on up here, and let's all talk about how we want this thing to go down."

He joined us at the leaning post. Robert pulled back a bit on the throttles so we could better carry on a conversation.

"Jim, what do you mean, *how we want it to go down*? I just want to kill the bastards!" Robert said.

"Yeah," I agreed. "But wouldn't that be murder?"

"Probably. But who cares? If they've hurt Georgia, I couldn't care less what the government thinks. I'll worry about that after I've blown their sorry heads off," Robert said.

"Yeah. But how are we going to know that?" I asked.

"They did it, Jim. If the girls aren't on the boat with them, if they aren't on that boat happily drinking beer, then I'm taking them out."

"OK," I said. "I'm with you, but exactly how are we going to do it?"

"Why don't we just wave them down?" Kenny asked.

"I'm OK with that," Robert agreed. "Jim, what do you think?"

"I'm OK with that, too, but, if the girls aren't on board, they're probably not going to stop. My guess is that they'll recognize your boat, know we are looking for them, and start to run like hell."

"Yep," Robert agreed. "We do need to see if the girls are aboard. If they start to run, then we start shooting."

"I'm OK with that," I said.

Then Kenny spoke up. "If we can run alongside them, I can take out their engines with this rifle. It'll be just like how the navy took out those Somali pirates a few years back. Then, once they are stopped, we can do what we have to do."

"That sounds good to me," Robert said. "Jim, you OK with that?"

"Yep," I said, looking to the west over the bow of the boat as I spoke. "And I reckon we better get ready. There's a boat coming our way."

After a few minutes, we could make out that it was a large blue center-console fishing boat. It was moving east, on a course reciprocal to ours. There was little doubt that this was the boat we were looking for.

"Robert," I asked. "Do you have any binoculars on board?"

"Yeah. Look up there in the electronics locker. I always keep a pair of Steiners handy—you know, just in case there might be a bikini-clad damsel in distress."

I just shook my head, then reached up in the bin. It took only a couple of swipes before my hand found the binocular case. The field glasses were indeed Steiners, one of the most expensive brands you can buy. I noted, as I took the binoculars out of the case, that their power was "seven x fifty." I remembered from my days in the army that the seven was a measure of magnification; the fifty indicated the diameter of the lens, which measures how much light can be gathered to form an image. *These should work fine*, I thought.

I put my elbows down against my chest and brought the lenses to my eyes. As I did that, I used my fingers to grip the binoculars while simultaneously forming a shield around the eyepieces to block outside light. This was another skill Uncle Sam had passed on to me many years ago.

I focused on the approaching boat. Even with the wide field of view from this quality optical device, it was difficult, given the bouncing of our boat, to keep the target in focus.

After a moment, Kenny could stand the suspense no longer. "Damn it, Jim. What do you see? Is it them? Are the girls on board?"

"It's R. V.'s boat, all right. I can tell that. It looks like two people are standing behind the console, but that's all I can see. We need to get closer."

As I said this, I could feel that Robert had adjusted our heading slightly, trying to make sure we were running exactly toward the other boat.

At that moment, we heard a noise off to the north and looked up to see an orange-and-white coast guard helicopter flying in the direction from which the approaching boat had just come. Seeing that chopper made me feel better. Now it was time for us to get down to our business.

Chapter Thirty-One

"Jill," Georgia asked, "are you OK?"

"My head's still above water, so I guess I'm all right. Are you OK? Roxie, how about you?"

Each responded positively.

"Thank God Shirley took pity on us," Jill said, struggling to speak as a wave broke over her face. "That guy with her was going to slit our throats."

"I guess she..." Georgia had to stop speaking, as her head momentarily slid beneath the sea. When she bobbed back up, she said, "I guess she appreciated that we had been kind to her."

"Pity, my ass," Roxie sputtered. "She was OK with feeding us to the sharks, wasn't she? My guess is that she just didn't want to see the sight of blood!"

At that moment, all three slid beneath the surface as a swell broke over them. A few seconds later, Jill came up, spitting saltwater. The other two surfaced a moment later, gasping for air.

"Girls," Jill said, "how far out do you think we are?"

"About fifty miles," Georgia replied. "It's damn sure too far to swim."

"How deep do you think it is?" Jill asked next.

"Well, I sure as hell can't touch!" Roxie replied.

At that, they all, between splutters, looked one another in the eyes, unsure of what they should say next. Instead, they just began to laugh.

Georgia, trying to keep the joke going, said, "Hey, come on, girls, it's really not all that deep. It's probably only about a hundred feet."

"Well, that's good!" Jill answered facetiously. "For a moment there I thought we might be in trouble."

"Possibly we could be," Roxie responded. "I guess it all depends on whether Nick was paying attention to my SPOT." Another wave forced them under.

When they all resurfaced, Georgia asked, "What the hell are you talking about, Roxie? What do you mean by it depends on whether he was paying attention to your SPOT? What kind of spot are you talking about? I didn't know y'all had that kind of relationship!"

"No! Not that kind of spot, Georgia. Get your mind out of the gutter. A SPOT is a personal-location beacon. It's kind of like a mini EPIRB, but you can carry it in your purse. All the girls in the office have them now for when we go out on calls. As soon as that creep came in, I grabbed it out of my bag, put it in my pocket, and switched on its tracking feature. Then, when they finally stopped out here and started to argue about whether to kill us, I mashed the SOS button. So, in theory, someone may be looking for us."

"In theory?" Jill responded.

"Well, if the damn thing works as well as the brochure claims," Roxie replied.

"Do you have it with you now?" Georgia asked.

"No," Roxie answered. "I knew it wouldn't work in the water, so I slipped it behind a life jacket that was stowed in the gunwale of the boat."

"Oh, crap!" Jill said dejectedly. "Doesn't that mean they'll start looking for the boat and not for us?"

"Maybe. But, you know, at the time, it seemed like a good idea. I didn't want them to find out I had it. If they had, they'd have turned it off, then dropped us off somewhere else. And they probably wouldn't have been as nice the next time. Nobody would have ever been able to find us, or our bodies, then. Now, at the very least, they'll be able to tell where the SOS was first activated. Hopefully, someone will think to look there."

"Hopefully!" Georgia and Jill replied jointly, just before ducking beneath the surface to dodge an oncoming whitecap.

"Georgia, do you know that guy who came in on us?" Roxie asked.

"He's from the East Coast. Unfortunately, we hadn't allowed for the fact that he might have a key to Shirley's house and that he might want to be there to surprise her when she returned from the doctor."

"Unfortunately!" Jill and Roxie replied before once again sinking beneath the sea.

When they'd all floated to the top, Jill said to Georgia, "You and that guy acted like y'all were acquainted."

"Yeah. I've met him a time or two with Robert, and he was at our party last month. I think he's a real estate appraiser for agricultural properties. He does a lot of work with growers in South Florida. And, I know he served as president of the Watermelon Association six or seven years ago."

"What's..." Roxie started to ask before she went under once again. Georgia waited patiently for her to resurface. "What's his name?" Roxie finally asked.

"Tony something or another," Georgia replied.

"Tony, as in Anthony?" Jill asked.

"I guess so," said Georgia. "But I've only ever heard him called Tony."

"So that could have been his ring Rachel found?" Jill said.

"Probably was," Georgia answered.

"Whoa! What was that?" Roxie asked.

"What was what?" Jill replied.

"I thought I saw some fins swimming by, out in that direction," Roxie said, pointing a hundred feet or so behind Jill and Georgia.

"Fins!" they screamed. "Fins, like shark fins?"

"Yeah."

Chapter Thirty-Two

Robert kept his boat pointing toward the bow of the approaching craft. With a combined closing speed of close to one hundred miles per hour, it didn't take long for the distance between the two vessels to narrow.

I kept the binoculars trained on the boat as the distance shrank. Finally, I said, "I only see two people on board, a man and a woman."

Neither Robert nor Kenny replied. But I could hear Kenny work the bolt on his rifle, ramming a cartridge into the firing chamber. I put the binoculars down and picked up one the twelve-gauges. Robert kept his eyes on the rapidly approaching boat. It wasn't until we were only maybe five hundred yards apart that the other boat reacted with a noticeable change of course, slightly toward the south. I smiled, thinking that the other captain had done exactly what was prescribed by the nautical rules of the road in order to avoid any chance of a collision. I'm pretty sure the other skipper had not anticipated, however, that Robert would then also change his heading—with the specific intent of maintaining a collision course. A few seconds later, the other boat, having seen this reaction, made another course correction. Robert, of course, did as well.

By now the two boats were only a couple of hundred yards apart and closing rapidly. The other skipper then cranked his wheel hard to starboard, obviously now concerned with the intent of the approaching vessel. Robert matched this course change, too. The process was repeated one last time. Now, the incoming boat was heading almost due south, and we were behind it, maybe only three hundred feet between us.

"Kenny," Robert said. "I think it's time to slow down that boat. You think you can take those engines out?"

Without a word, Kenny leaned his shoulder against one of the aluminum posts that supported the T-top, and aimed at the fleeing craft's starboard-most engine. A second later, just as our boat rolled crossing a swell, we heard an explosive *crack* as Kenny fired the high-powered weapon. We all looked expectantly toward the boat in front to see if he'd managed to take out one of the engines. But we were disappointed to see no obvious sign of damage.

"Shit!" Kenny exclaimed, as he manipulated the bolt to position another round in the chamber. Again, he carefully braced himself, aimed the rifle, and squeezed the trigger. When we looked forward to survey the destruction, we could see no indication that the boat had been struck.

What we *could* see was that the boat we were chasing had reacted by pushing down its throttles as far as they would go. Robert answered in kind, and now we were bouncing from wave top to wave top. We noticed that the boat we were chasing was behaving the same.

"Kenny," Robert yelled disgustedly. "When was the last time you shot a rifle?"

"Well, I used to shoot a twenty-two back when I was a kid—you know, when I was rabbit hunting."

"That's what I thought. Jim, you take the controls and get us as close as you can. Kenny, give me that damn Winchester."

Robert moved to the starboard side of the boat, took a relaxed and balanced position with his feet spread widely apart, chambered a round, and shouldered the weapon. I noticed him tracking the quarry in front, apparently trying to get a feel for how it was moving in relationship to our boat. Finally, as our boat momentarily stabilized itself on the top of a swell, Robert fired.

This time there was no doubt that we had scored a hit. Smoke had begun to pour from the cowling of the starboard engine. We also noticed that the boat ahead had slowed slightly. Consequently, we were able to quickly close the distance. Robert assumed his firing position again. As he did, the boat ahead began to weave from side to side, but we were so close now that it was almost impossible for him to miss. His second shot took out the port engine, leaving only the center engine still operating. Of course, with this strike, the boat's speed slowed even more dramatically. A few seconds later, following a third shot, flames began to pour from the remaining engine. The pursued vessel slowed to a stop.

"Jim, give me a damned shotgun," Robert ordered.

By this time, I had throttled back our engines. Now, we were slowly approaching the stricken craft. I looked carefully to see what the man and woman on board were up to. Specifically, I studied their hands. The last thing I wanted was for them to pull out their own guns and begin to shoot at us. As soon as we were within fifty feet, I began to circle the stricken boat. By this time, there was no doubt that the woman on board was Shirley Dodge. I recognized the man, too. He was the guy who had taken R. V.'s side during the argument at Bruce's party.

All the while that we were circling, Robert had his semiautomatic Remington trained directly at the man's head. Kenny, on the other hand, had picked up the rifle and had it pointed in the general direction of the other boat.

Robert then bellowed across the water, "Tony, what'd you do with Georgia?"

The man answered, "Robert Parrish, have you lost your mind? I don't know anything about your wife. Shirley and I were just out fishing. Can't you see the damn rods on the rocket launchers? You're going to pay for this mess, Parrish. And I'm going to see that you're prosecuted, too."

I don't know what kind of response the man had been expecting, but I doubt he'd anticipated a solid pattern of buckshot exploding the electronics locker directly over his head.

"Robert! Goddamn it, stop shooting!" Shirley Dodge hollered. "We didn't hurt Georgia and the others. We just threw them into the water. I didn't want to harm them. I just wanted to teach them a lesson about breaking into my house. They were all OK the last time we saw them. We can give you the coordinates where we dropped them."

Shirley probably wasn't expecting the shot pattern that came in her direction, either. This time it took out most of the leaning post on which she had propped herself. As soon as it disintegrated, she yelled, "Damn you, Robert. I told you I'd give you their location. You hurt me or Tony, and you'll never find them!"

This time Robert blew a hole the size of a dinner plate in the hull of the boat, right at the waterline.

Now Shirley started to scream. "Robert, I can't swim. Please don't sink this boat. For God's sake, take pity on us."

While all of this had been going down, I had been focusing on the fishing rods sticking up from the rod holders on the stern of R. V.'s boat. I guess I might have been looking at them because I didn't really want to see what Robert was going to do next. As I looked at the rods, it finally dawned on me what I had been missing all this time. Specifically, all of R. V.'s grouper rods were rigged using standard neon-orange plastic beads, exactly the same color and pattern of beads that had been used in the grouper rig to sew R. V.'s mouth shut. As this dawned on me, I recalled that Mack Emory never used beads of that color when he created his fishing rigs. I remembered that, in memory of his grandfather, he only used a unique, unvarying, pattern of green and red beads. To me that was proof, as if we needed it at this point, that Mack Emory hadn't killed R. V. Now, if we could get out of this situation without being charged with murder ourselves, I'd have to remember to point this discrepancy out to Mike Collins.

This realization brought me back to the situation unfolding in front of us. "Robert," I asked softly, "What's your plan?" I could see Kenny watching both of us intently, worried I suspected about how all of this was going to play out.

Robert replied in a low voice, "Those two pieces of crap up there threw our wives into the damn ocean. There are sharks out there that are longer than this boat. And those scumbags are hoping right now, I'm sure, that those sharks have already eaten the girls so there'll be no one left to implicate them. That way, it'll just be their word against ours. I don't intend to give them the opportunity to use that strategy."

"Robert," I said, "I don't want them to get away with it, either. But maybe we should just wait a little bit to hear if the coast guard was able to find the girls. If the girls are OK, we won't need to kill these guys."

"Maybe, but they've only got five minutes." He fired another round into the waterline of the boat. By now it was starting to sit noticeably lower in the water. That gave me an idea.

"Shirley," I yelled. "Why'd you throw the girls in the water? Why didn't you just kill them first, then throw them in?"

"That's what we should have done with them!" Tony replied.

"Shut up, Tony," Shirley yelled. "This whole mess is your fault, anyway. I wouldn't let Tony kill them like he wanted to. He was going to slit their throats and feed them to the sharks, but those girls have been too nice to me since Tony killed R. V. I wanted to at least give them a chance. That's why I let them jump in the water."

"I appreciate that, Shirley," I said. "I really do. That was kind of you. And I'll make sure I ask the prosecutor to take that into consideration. That is, if Robert lets you live. You know, he's pretty pissed off right now about what you did to Georgia." As I said that, I winked at Robert with the eye Shirley could not see.

"Oh, for God's sake, you can't let him kill me. All of this was Tony's idea, not mine. If it had been just up to me, I'd have let the girls go. I really would have."

"I'm sure you would have, Shirley," I replied.

"You stupid bitch!" was Tony's concise reply. "You're just like R. V. Neither one of you ever knew how to keep your damn mouth shut!"

Shirley opened her mouth to reply but was unable to actually say anything due to the deafening interruption from five rapidly fired twelve-gauge blasts. Robert, apparently having gotten tired of listening to Shirley blame Tony for her problems, had used his weapon to open a much more sizable hole in the waterline of their boat. Consequently, it was now rapidly filling with water, the stern already beginning to sink beneath the surface.

Shirley had begun to scream. I couldn't make out what she was saying, even though she was certainly saying it loudly. Tony was glaring at Robert.

"All right, children," Robert said. "I promised Jim we'd wait five minutes to see if the girls were all right before I killed you. Well, guess what? Your five minutes are up."

He lifted the big gun to his shoulder and drew a steady bead on Tony's head.

"Wait a minute," I said quickly. "I've got a better idea. You don't need to shoot them. We can just make them do the same thing they made the girls do. Their boat's sinking. As soon as it goes down and they jump in the water, we'll leave them. Then we go out and find the girls."

"OK, I can buy that. Actually, I like it. We'll give them a dose of their own medicine."

"Exactly! It'll kind of be like karma," I replied.

"Yeah! And, karma can be a bitch," Robert said, laughing tersely.

As we watched, the big center console began to slide beneath the sea. In what seemed like only seconds, the boat had turned over so that the hull was now upmost, and the bow was the only part of the boat still sticking out of the water. Shirley and Tony had both leaped clear, as the boat had begun to twist upside down as it sank.

I had my eye on the two people in the water. I actually didn't want either of them to drown. If they really couldn't swim, I was prepared to intervene.

Kenny apparently had been watching, too. "Hey, guys, it looks like Shirley can swim after all."

As we watched, she was performing a weak, but effective, free-style crawl, moving rapidly away from where Tony was silently, and sullenly, treading water.

"You know, Robert," Kenny continued, "seeing a pretty boat sinking like that is a damn sad sight. It's tearing me up. I think you need to put it out of its misery."

"I can do that." Robert forcefully slapped in a new magazine, racked the weapon to chamber a shell, raised the heavy-barreled gun, and sent a salvo of five rapidly squeezed-off shots into the upraised bow. The impact of the concentrated buckshot pattern punched a hole in the hull, which allowed the trapped air, the only thing still keeping the boat afloat, to escape. As it did, it made a loud whooshing sound and sent a tall plume of spray spewing into the sky. The scene reminded me of a whale breeching. Then the boat sank completely into the sea. The only things still visible in the water were the two swimmers, the desperation of their situations now beginning to show on their faces.

"Well," I said, "we better get going if we're going to find the girls."

Chapter Thirty-Three

"Roxie," screamed Georgia. "Are you sure you saw shark fins?"

"That's what they looked like to me. I don't think it's likely that dolphins would be out this far."

"Ladies," Jill said. "This is starting to get serious. What do you think we should do?"

"For starters, I think we ought to huddle together," Roxie said. "Maybe the sharks will be afraid of a bigger target."

"Yeah," said Georgia. "Or maybe they'll just get more excited about the possibility of a bigger meal."

"Georgia, damn it," Jill exploded. "You just shut up. We are not going to be eaten by sharks. That's just not going to happen."

"OK! Sorry. I was just trying to lighten the mood," Georgia apologized.

"Georgia, I'm sorry," Jill said. "I guess I'm starting to get a little tense. Is there anything else we can do?"

"I guess we can try to pray," Roxie ventured.

"I've already got that covered," Jill said. "I've been praying since that guy came in on us, but I might be a little bit out of practice. It hasn't seemed to help yet."

"Well, whatever you do, don't stop," Georgia responded. "Maybe his line's just been busy."

For the next several minutes, none of the girls spoke. Each was facing away from the group, intently scanning the surface for additional fins. Fortunately, they hadn't seen any; however, the sharks could easily have swum by during the several times the girls were submerged by cresting waves.

Finally, Georgia could no longer stand the silence; she spoke up through her salt-encrusted lips. "Girls, I'm sorry I got you into this mess. I really am. I was just trying to have a little bit of fun, but I guess it's not very funny right now."

"It'll be fun to talk about after we get out of this," Roxie replied.

"Yeah," Jill and Georgia replied quietly. But, truthfully, at that moment, neither of them was feeling particularly amused. And they were even less amused when the next large whitecap, a wave larger than any they'd yet had to deal with, broke on them.

When they'd resurfaced and had rubbed the stinging salt from their eyes, Georgia said, "Girls, I don't want us to get morbid or anything, but just to pass the time, assuming we don't get out of this situation, what will y'all miss most about your lives?"

Jill responded, "Of course we're going to get out of this. But, hypothetically speaking, should we not, I think I'd most miss my kids and my grandkids. I'd miss being with them as they lived out their lives. I'd miss that a lot. And, of course, I'd miss being with Jim, too. How about you, Georgia? What would you miss?"

"I'd miss Robert, and my friends. And I'd really miss cooking."

"You do cook well, Georgia," Jill responded. "I'd miss your cooking, too. Roxie, how about you? What would you miss most?"

"Damn it, girls! We aren't going to miss anything. One way, or another, we're going to get out of this mess. Watch out—wave's coming."

The swell swamped them, preventing further immediate conversation. When they bobbed back up, Jill said, "Oh, come on, Roxie! Lighten up. We know we're going to get out of this, but we've got to do something to pass the time. What would you miss?"

"Will y'all shut up and listen for a minute? I think I just heard something!"

They all listened intently. Jill finally spoke, "I do sort of hear something, too. It sounds like a beating sound, maybe. Do y'all hear it?"

"Oh! Oh!" Georgia said. "I think...I think...it's a helicopter. That's what it sounds like to me. Maybe the coast guard's coming for us."

All three paddled to turn themselves and look in the direction from which the sound was coming. Still, it took almost a minute before they could finally see the chopper.

"There it is!" Roxie said, pointing excitedly to the northeast. "Do you see it?"

"I can see something," Jill responded. "It's down low to the water. It looks like they're searching for us."

"Oh, I see it, too!" Georgia said. "They are looking for us, but crap— they're looking in the wrong place."

"Oh, Lord. Make them come this way!" Jill cried. "Let's all splash, and maybe they'll be able to see us."

All three started to wave their arms and kick their feet. Soon they were thrashing for all they were worth, but for two or three long minutes, the chopper continued to slowly work its search pattern, showing no sign *of having seen them. By this time, the girls were not only splashing, but also screaming at the top of their lungs.*

"Damn you, can't you see us? Open your eyes. Please! We're over here," hollered Roxie.

For her part, Georgia was just emitting a loud yell, "Whooee, Whooee, Whooee!"

Jill was alternating between cussing and pleading.

***

Finally, just as they were beginning to despair of ever being seen, the copter abruptly changed course and began to fly in their direction. As it got nearer, the girls could see a dayglow-orange, wet-suit-clad figure standing at the side door of the chopper. He waved, then looked down attentively at them. All three ladies waved back, and Roxie blew him a kiss. They could see the airman laugh at that.

As the craft hovered overhead, the rescue swimmer maneuvered a wire basket outside the helicopter and slid into it quickly. Soon the basket was descending toward them. They could see a small line dangling beneath the basket into the water. Georgia started to swim toward the line, but the airman motioned for her to not touch the line.

"I think that's a static-discharge line," Jill said. "I saw that on TV one time. Don't touch it, or you may be electrocuted."

"OK. I won't touch it. I won't get near it!" Georgia answered. "But thank God they came for us."

As Georgia and Jill finished this conversation, Roxie, shaking off the shock of having been lost at sea, began excitedly whispering, "Damn, he's good-looking. I don't think I've seen a man with muscles like that in twenty years. I'm pretty sure I'm in love!"

Jill laughed at her, and then answered, "Roxie, let's just worry about getting out of this damn water and into the helicopter. Then you can hit on him!"

At that moment, the rescue swimmer jumped from the basket into the sea and began to swim strongly toward the ladies. As he approached, he carefully looked at each of them and questioned them about their conditions.

Satisfied that there were no critical issues to resolve, he calmly said: "All right, ladies, we're going to have you all out of here in a couple of minutes. I'm going to help you, one at a time, into the basket and then you'll be lifted to the helicopter. Who wants to go first?"

Roxie spoke up quickly, "Those two need to go first. They're in much weaker condition than I am. I'm very worried about them. I'll stay in the water with you until they are on board."

Jill and Georgia looked at each other knowingly, and rolled their eyes.

"That's OK with me," said the airman. "So which of you two wants to go first?"

"Georgia, you go ahead," said Jill. "I'll wait with Roxie."

Less than a minute later, Georgia was aboard the chopper, and the basket was being lowered once again. Jill made the next trip, and then it was Roxie's turn. The swimmer, with his basket, was the last to come on board.

A medic on the helicopter immediately took charge of each one getting into the chopper. He provided towels for them to use to dry off, then helped wrap each of them in a thermal blanket to provide immediate warmth. While he did this, he carefully questioned them about how they were feeling.

With Georgia, he didn't even have time to get through all his planned queries before she put an end to them by giving him an affectionate hug and exclaiming, "Damn, are we glad to see you boys! Thank you, thank you, thank you for coming to get us. And you don't have to ask me all your silly questions. I'm fine."

When Jill came on board, her reaction was only slightly less appreciative. She, too, hugged the medic and thanked him profusely.

The airman, for his part, took the displays of affection in stride and immediately concluded that the first two ladies were OK. He professionally dealt with their needs, and then turned to await the arrival of the last survivor. As it turned out, Roxie's entrance was a good deal more dramatic.

As she stepped out of the basket, she grabbed her chest and swayed a little from side to side. "Oh, it's my heart!" she exclaimed, before adding, "I'm not feeling very well. It could be my heart, it could be my blood pressure, and I'm having trouble breathing."

Jill, however, couldn't help but notice that all the time Roxie was complaining, she was also glancing out the door of the chopper to keep a close eye on the progress being made by the ascending rescue swimmer. Jill knew then there was really no reason to worry about Roxie. But, she thought to herself, the muscular airman riding the basket toward the chopper might have some reason to be concerned. Jill looked at Georgia. They again rolled their eyes and smiled. The attentive medic, having noticed them do this, laughed, winked, and smiled, too.

Chapter Thirty-Four

Robert took a moment to plot a course to where we thought the girls were likely to be. Kenny was discarding into the gulf spent shotgun shells from the deck. I was stowing the weapons.

"'Big Melons,' 'Big Melons,' Lee County Sheriff. Come in, 'Big Melons.'"

Robert snatched the microphone from its hook and replied, "Lee County, 'Big Melons.' What you got?"

"'Big Melons,' go to channel seventy-six."

Seconds later, we were on the sheriff's working channel and heard the following, "'Big Melons,' we've got the ladies. They're OK. Over."

"They're all OK? Over," Robert said.

"We think so," Mike Collins replied. "The real estate lady is complaining of some mild chest pains, but the medic doesn't think it's anything serious. He says the other two seem fine. Over."

"Where are they, Mike? Over."

"They're on the coast guard's chopper. They're flying to the helipad at Lee Memorial Hospital. If you want, I can have a deputy meet y'all at the Sanibel dock. He'll drive y'all there."

"Perfect. We can be there in about thirty minutes. Over."

"Have y'all seen anything of the boat we were looking for? The one that dropped the ladies in the gulf? Over."

Robert looked at Kenny and me. We all knew this was an important question. I looked into Robert's eyes and nodded.

Robert pressed the microphone switch and replied to the sheriff. "That boat you've been looking for just sank. The two individuals who were on it are now treading water in the gulf. You need the last location for the boat? Over."

"No. We've got it from the SPOT. Our chopper should be there in about seven minutes. What caused the boat to sink? Over."

"Looked to us like it suddenly developed a few leaks," Robert replied. "Mike, if your guys are on the way, I don't see any reason for us to stick around any longer. We're on the way to Sanibel. Over and out."

Robert quickly punched some buttons to set a course for Redfish Pass. He then brought the boat around to that heading and slammed the throttles down, bringing the boat onto a fast plane. As we sped past the two heads bobbing, uncomfortably and worriedly, in the sea, Kenny and I waved. I noticed that Robert was even more emphatic as he shot them a couple of energetically delivered middle-finger salutes. I looked back one last time, just as the wake from our boat broke over their heads. I could see them still bobbing in the water, but not much else, as behind them the rays of the sun, now organizing itself for its nightly descent into the depths of the gulf, made vision difficult. But, farther out I saw what I thought might have been several large fins slowly and silently slicing through the now darkening water of the gulf. Of course, given the glare, it's possible that I might have just been imagining things.

Chapter Thirty-Five

Twenty eight minutes later, Robert and I hopped out of the boat and onto the county's dock in Sanibel. We were greeted by an anxious-looking deputy. We'd already arranged for Kenny to take the boat back to Robert's house, and for Janice to meet him there. The deputy's squad car, its lights flashing brightly in the fading light, stood at the foot of the pier, ready to whisk Robert and me to the hospital in downtown Fort Myers. We jogged toward it, not wasting time on exchanging pleasantries with the deputy. The officer began running, too. He quickly buckled himself in the driver's seat, as Robert and I slid onto the hard plastic bench in the back.

The deputy glanced in his rearview mirror to see if we were ready to travel. In response, Robert answered through the extruded metal screen that separated us from the driver: "Come on, man, you're wasting time. We're in a hurry."

That was all the encouragement the deputy needed. He flipped a switch to activate the car's loud siren, jammed the throttle to the floor, and fishtailed out of the paved parking lot, leaving behind a cloud of smoke, and two thick stripes of black rubber.

Satisfied that the deputy was doing all he could to get us downtown as quickly as possible we sat back in our seats, and gripped whatever we could to keep from sliding around.

As soon as I had become convinced that the officer knew enough about driving to not kill us, I turned to Robert and asked him: "All right, Robert, what in the heck were Shirley and that guy Tony up to? Why'd they kill R. V., and why'd they try to kill the girls? I want the whole truth this time. Don't leave anything out."

Robert looked me in the eyes, nodded his head up and down, as if silently agreeing to do what I had asked, and said: "Tony, or more formally, Richard Anthony Porter Jr., is in cahoots with Asa Parsons. Tony's the appraiser who worked with the Parsons brothers when they sold their land to the state. Together they've cooked up a scheme to fund Asa's run for governor. Essentially, if a large agricultural landowner who owns property anywhere near the watershed that flows down into Lake Okeechobee agrees to make a large donation to Parsons and to the party, then Asa will see that the South Florida Water Management District, for which he currently sits as a board member, will buy a conservation easement on as much of the property that the land owner wants to sell. Of course, the appraised price of that property—through the efforts of Tony and his buddies—will be vastly inflated. Maybe three to four times what the land is actually worth. The standard arrangement is for the land owner to donate ten percent of the estimated easement price to Parsons, and for the appraisers to each get a couple of hundred grand under the table. It's a slick deal."

"So, why was R. V. killed? It sounds to me like something that he would have been in favor of."

"Oh, he was that, for sure! But, he could never keep his mouth shut. He was always trying to convince others to jump on board and get some of the gravy for themselves. And, you know how R. V. was. He couldn't do anything quietly. I don't know for sure, but I suspect that was why Tony killed him. He was concerned that someone who shouldn't know about the deal would overhear R. V. bragging about it."

"Robert, are you in on the deal, too?"

"No. Probably should be. If I had, it would have made me and my family a lot of money. But, every time that I'd think about doing it, I'd think about the two things my daddy taught me about how you should behave. He always said to think about how you'd feel if what you were doing was going to be on the front page of the newspaper. And, he always advised me to think about what my mama would think about what you were doing. I don't think that Mama would have liked this deal very much."

"Probably not," I agreed.

We rode the rest of the way to the hospital in silence.

Chapter Thirty-Six

As we pulled into the main entrance to Lee Memorial, the deputy thoughtfully silenced the siren. But, he left the car's strobe lights on. Consequently, as we wheeled toward the front door of the hospital, we got more than a few stares from folks walking to, and from, their vehicles.

The deputy had planned to drop us at the hospital's main visitor's entrance, but as we came around the driveway leading in that direction I yelled at him to stop.

"Take us over there," I directed, pointing in the direction of the right side of the building where two bedraggled-looking women were sitting on a bench. Another sheriff's cruiser was sitting nearby, with neither lights nor siren drawing attention, but with a bulky, heavily muscled officer leaning comfortably against its fender, attentively keeping watch on the two females.

"Man," Robert said. "They're not looking too good."

"A little worse for wear," I agreed. "But, from the looks of what they're drinking, I'd say that they are probably going to be all right."

Robert looked closer and began to laugh. Each lady had a tall can of beer in her hands. Two empties were in a plastic bag on the ground, and two more, still surrounded by plastic rings, waited on the bench to be pressed into service.

Our driver calmly maneuvered behind the other squad car and parked. We all got out. Robert and I went directly to the girls, while our driver walked to the far side of the other cruiser and motioned for the other deputy to join him there. I appreciated them trying to give us a little privacy.

As soon as the ladies recognized us, they leapt to their feet, and ran to embrace us. As soon as we'd hugged and kissed, Robert and I both held the girls out at arms' length so that we could get a better look at their conditions.

"Are y'all OK?" I asked.

As I said that, I could see both of the ladies self-consciously attempting to push hair out of their faces and smooth down the wrinkles in their still-damp clothes.

"Y'all stop that!" Robert commanded. "You look great to us."

That's for sure," I agreed. "Now, seriously, are y'all OK?"

"We are now that Officer Scott took us down to the convenience store and bought us a six-pack. The man deserves a commendation!"

"It sounds like you're OK," I said. "What the hell happened?"

Georgia began to tell the tale. "It was my fault, I guess. I got the girls to go with me to see if we could find out who was having an affair with Shirley. We figured that if we could do that, then we'd also know who had killed R. V. But, we hadn't counted on Tony having a key and catching us red-handed. He had a knife, and he kept us until Shirley came home. He wanted to kill us there, but Shirley talked him out of doing that. Anyway, they decided to load us onto R. V.'s boat and take us out into the gulf. They figured that if the dumped us out there, no one would ever know what had happened to us. Thank God that Roxy had her SPOT. And, thank God that Jill was able to convince Shirley to spare our lives!"

"You convinced her not to kill you?" I asked Jill. "How'd you do that?"

"Well, that's not really what happened. But, when Tony took Georgia and Roxy out to the boat I was alone with Shirley for a few minutes, and I talked to her. It was all I could do."

"So, what'd you say to her?" I asked.

"I asked her if she and Tony had killed R. V. When she said that they had, I asked her why. She said it was because she and Tony were in love. At that, I looked her in the eyes and told her that from how I'd just heard him talking to Shirley, I didn't think that Tony was in love. Then I suggested that it was just probably because of the money. From the look on her face when I said that, I could tell that it wasn't the first time that she had thought about that. I guess that was enough to make her reconsider the wisdom of killing us. But, for whatever reason, she kept Tony from slitting out throats us when we were in the gulf. If she hadn't done that we wouldn't be here."

"Yeah, that's for sure," I agreed. "Where's Roxy? How's she doing?"

At that, Georgia and Jill looked at each other and began to laugh.

"Well," Jill said, "Georgia was trying to hit on the rescue swimmer who pulled us from the gulf. To ensure that he examined her carefully she feigned experiencing a little shortness of breath, and having some mild chest pains. As a result, she's now being kept overnight for observation. But, we've been released."

"Serves her right," Robert said.

"But," Georgia replied, "From what I overheard, the airman told Roxy that he would stop by the hospital after he was off duty to check on her. I suspect that right now she's up there trying to select the most attractive hospital gown she can find."

"She could always wear it backward," Robert said.

We all laughed in agreement.

"Y'all ready to be taken home?" our deputy asked.

"We sure are!" I said. "With lights and sirens all the way."

Made in the USA
Charleston, SC
03 January 2017